OF MASQUERADES & FAME

CANDICE PEDRAZA YAMNITZ
CLAIRE KOHLER

The story, all names, characters, and incidents portrayed in this production are fictitious. No identification with actual persons (living or deceased), places, buildings, and products is intended or should be inferred.

Cover and interior design by Candice Pedraza Yamnitz

Illustrations by Candice Pedraza Yamnitz First edition 2025 Names: Yamnitz, Candice Pedraza, author

Title: Of Masquerades and Fame/ Candice Pedraza Yamnitz and Claire Kohler

Description: Audience: Ages 13+. | Summary: In the aftermath of the infamous Sky Manor game, 18-year-old Camilla Carranza receives an invitation to the Elite Ball, the place where the most lucrative business deals transpire. Despite her boyfriend's misgivings, Camilla accepts the invitation, thinking it will lead to enough money for her and Rupert to finally get married. She doesn't realize she's walking into a sinister trap where the only way to survive may be by returning to the past she swore she'd left behind.
Rupert Nelson's love for Camilla withstood the testing in the Sky Manor game but loving her and trusting her are two different things. When he discovers she's gone behind his back to the Elite Ball, he sneaks in to rescue her, only to realize this is the perfect chance to determine her true loyalty.
In a dance of opulence and lies, will Camilla and Rupert's escape from the Elite cost them everything-even the love they're so desperate to protect?

ISBN: 979-8-9997479-0-7 (paperback)

Subjects: Young Adult -- Fiction. | Mystery and Detective -- Fiction. | Teen & Young Adult Fantasy

"Take care, and be on your guard against all
covetousness, for one's life does not consist in the
abundance of his possessions."
Luke 12:15 (ESV)

REMAINING SKY MANOR COMPETITORS

RUPERT NELSON

THE EX-SMUGGLER

CAMILLA CARRANZA

THE EX-GOLD DIGGER

ZENITH LAURUS

THE EX-ASSASSIN

MAPLE HILL

OWNER OF THE
SCREAMING PEACH CAFE

JESSIE SMITH

THE EX-THIEF

The New Players

HORACE AMBROSE

THE GOVERNOR'S SON

WES ACTON

LADY ARABELLA'S STEPSON

LADY ARABELLA

LADY OF THE ACTON ESTATE

FLORA WOODHOUSE

FORMER ZEPPELIN PILOT

MR. WOODHOUSE

SKY MANOR BUTLER

PHOENIX LAZARUS

ZENITH'S MOTHER

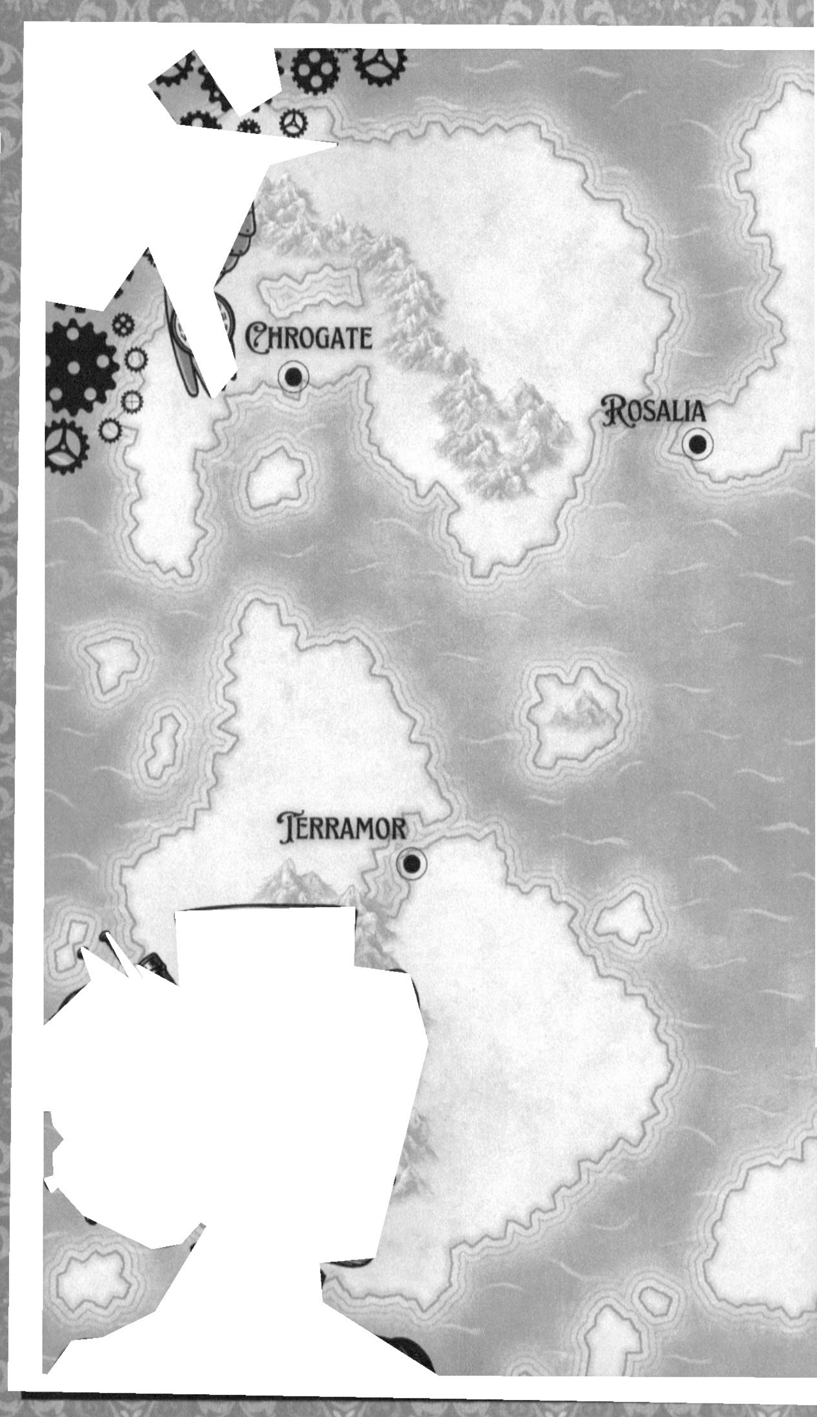

CHROGATE
ROSALIA
TERRAMOR

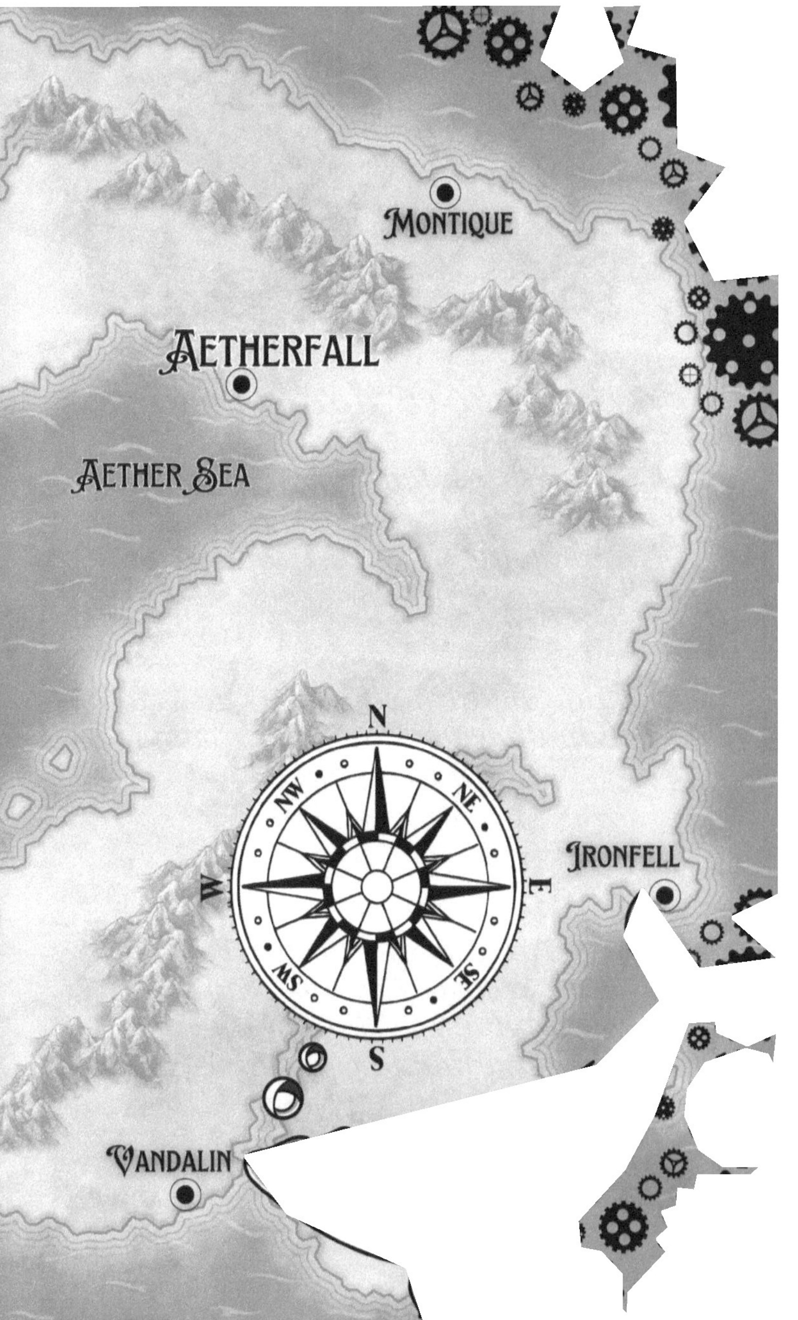

MONTIQUE
ÆTHERFALL
ÆTHER SEA
IRONFELL
N
NW
NE
W
E
SW
SE
S
VANDALIN

You are cordially invited

to an
Exclusive Masquerade Ball
at the Acton Estate
A night of mystery, elegance, and
enchantment

Indulge in fine dining, live music, and
enchanting entertainment throughout
the evening.

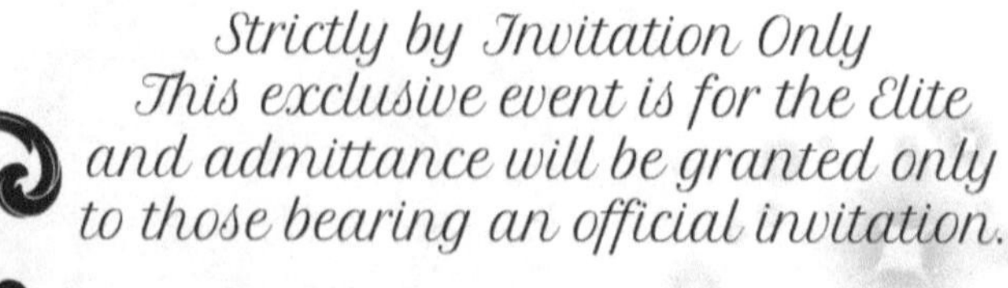

Strictly by Invitation Only
This exclusive event is for the Elite
and admittance will be granted only
to those bearing an official invitation.

Prologue

CAMILLA

THE DAY I FOUND out that I was one of the *blessed* would become the scar on my life that never healed.

When I was seven years old, my nine-year-old sister, Maria, and I waited at the soda shop after school pretending we could afford the drinks served in fancy-looking bottles. An automaton wiped the counters with its pipe arms while a man prepared special drinks. I fixed my uniform dress and kicked my school sack beneath the counter to keep it hidden—no one should see the ratty thing my parents made me use.

"What will you two girls be ordering today?" The bushy-eyebrowed man asked from behind the counter.

Maria giggled—far too suspiciously. "We're still deciding."

The man's round eyes arched with wariness, but he didn't throw us out. "Let me know when you're ready." The man pointed off behind us to a line of students formed at the doorway. "Try not to take too long."

He wiped the counter with a white rag and organized the curvy glass bottles he used to serve beverages.

Everyone who was anyone at school showed up to the soda shop on Main Street while walking home from our private school. We had gotten a scholarship to attend from an unnamed donor. But Maria had her suspicion of whom it could be.

"Come on." Maria hopped off the stool and snatched my wrist. "It's the Lady Arabella."

"My sack." I lunged for my bag that held my literature books, which I'd snuck from the class shelves to read before they were assigned. It was the only way to stay ahead in school. I snatched my bag and skipped over to Maria's side.

Maria gave me her annoyed look, the one where she wrinkled her pixie nose and glared at me. She was convinced that Lady Arabella was our donor. She found Maria and I adorable because we were cute and had learned our manners. Mamá came from a wealthy family across the isles but had fallen in love with

Papá when she'd visited Aetherfall City. I loved my family, but coins were always in want.

Lady Arabella turned into the mask and hat shop. I wasn't sure what we'd do while following her, but Maria was obsessed with the idea of showing our donor her money was going to good use.

We peeked through the store window adorned with giant fluffy feathers sticking out the tops of hats, and lace everywhere. A line of sparkling masks blinked at me from the other side of the window. Though the day was cloud-covered and no sun peeked through to make our day happy, those masks were the most beautiful things I had ever seen. Yet, I had no idea when anyone would have a chance to wear them.

"Let's go inside." Maria tiptoed into the shop.

I yanked my hand back, suddenly feeling out of place. The soda shop was one thing, but a store with polished wood and gem-encrusted goods was another. "Let's go home."

"We can't arrive too early, or we'll never be able to play after school again." Maria crossed her arms and tapped her hole-patched, black shoes. She knew she had me there.

Mamá would grow suspicious of why we'd arrived so early and find out we'd taken detours every day from school. If Mamá started picking us up with the babies wrapped around her body and my booger-picking little sister at the school, the other girls would never let Maria and me live down our shame.

"Fine."

Maria opened the shop door. The bell above us rang so loud that both the lady and the storekeeper whipped their heads toward us.

"Aww . . . why, hello, girls." Lady Arabella adjusted her face into a warm smile. "Would you like to help me choose a mask for the ball tonight?"

"Yes," Maria and I shouted at the same time. We ran over to the counter, where the storekeeper laid out five masks. The scent of leather and flowers mingled together into the most glorious thing I'd ever sniffed.

Though the sparkle glimmered under the shopkeeper's gaslamps, I couldn't help staring at Lady Arabella. She had long hair twisted into a bun at the top of her head and pearls wrapped around her neck. Mamá only wore necklaces on special occasions, but they were so pretty. Why not wear them every day?

Maria pushed me off to the side, which sparked a flame within my stomach. Why did she always get to do the fun things? I would have pushed back, but Mamá reminded me all the time that sweet little girls shouldn't fight, especially if they wanted to find a dashing prince for a husband. I patted down my school dress and caught sight of Lady Arabella's open purse. A shiny glass bottle like the ones in the soda shop called to me. It said: *Open me, drink me, see that I am good.*

Everything in me screamed that this was wrong. I shouldn't steal. Yet, I had never tasted soda before, and the bottle was so beautiful.

Without thinking it through, I grabbed the item and stuffed it in my sack.

At the same time, Maria tried on a mask and Lady Arabella fit one to her own face. They both laughed, but I wouldn't budge from my spot as they continued. Should I put the bottle back? Lady Arabella didn't know I'd taken it yet. Then again, if I got caught returning it, she'd know I'd stolen it, and we might lose our scholarship.

Guilt built up so high into my throat that I thought I might scream the truth and cry my way out of this.

"Thank you, darling, for helping me choose a mask for tonight." Lady Arabella patted Maria's head. The three of us walked out together and waved goodbye. Lady Arabella headed into the city, and we walked the opposite direction. The bustle of people and automatons on the stone walkway silenced any conversation between my older sister and me.

When we crossed into the Yellow District, Maria stopped at a park bench. "One day, I'm going to be invited to one of those balls and buy myself a mask like that one."

I sat beside her and took out the bottle.

"Where did you get that?"

Heat flamed my cheeks. "I don't know."

"Camilla"—Maria said my name like a sharp slap to the face—"did you steal it from the soda shop?"

I nodded vigorously, not wanting her to know it was from Lady Arabella's purse.

"Don't do that again." Maria wagged her finger at me. "But I kind of wanted a taste of the soda, too."

The cool glass on my palm dazzled with promise. I popped the cork with Maria's permission and drank a gulp. The sweet flavor tickled my tongue, drained into my throat, and filled me with the best feeling ever.

"Let me try it." Maria grabbed the glass from my hands, which I hated, but since she wasn't going to tell Mamá about me stealing, I let her take the drink without a fight. She sipped the liquid and took a gulp.

"That's too much."

She extended her arm, keeping me away and almost finishing the bottle. "See, I left you some."

"I hate you." The scornful words left my mouth despite me loving Maria most of all.

"Here! Take your drink, complainer."

I yanked the bottle from her hands and finished the last of the pink beverage, which was more than I'd assumed would be left—but never got a chance to tell Maria that.

"My belly hurts," Maria said.

"It's because you drank everything."

We marched home with Maria groaning. That was when I should have known something was wrong. Maria never would have let me get away with my exaggerated comment on any other occasion.

I stuffed the bottle in my bag again. The tickle inside of me felt good and brought an extra kick to my step.

The two of us stopped in front of the little gate around our house. She pinned me down with this odd look, then bent over and vomited all over the walkway. I opened the gate and ran to get Mamá. When Mamá came out of the front door, she handed me my baby brother to carry and brought Maria into our tiny home.

That night, I slipped under the covers beside Maria. She moaned and groaned all night, filling a basin far more times than I'd ever seen before. I spun over on my bed, unsure if I should tell Mamá about the bottle I'd stolen. We'd both drunk Lady Arabella's drink, but I hadn't gotten sick.

Mamá remained by the bedside on a small stool, wearing a deep frown line atop her forehead.

Papá entered the room. "Should we call a doctor?"

"Yes." Mamá's voice came out wispy, unlike the strong tone she always used. A knot formed in my heart and pulsed with worry.

When the old doctor came into the room and examined my sister, Maria looked the color of a pearl under the oil lamp Mamá held.

"Has she eaten anything different?" the doctor asked.

"Not that I know of." Mamá set her attention on me. "Camilla, do you know?"

A shiver ran across my skin.

"Camilla, what did she eat?" It was like Mamá could see right through me.

I climbed out of the bed and grabbed the small bottle from my sack. I extended my trembling arm out to Mamá.

"What is this?" Mamá snatched the bottle and examined the glass as if she could produce an answer from the clear material.

The doctor then took the vial and popped the cork open. He put it up to his nose and inhaled deeply. "Poison."

Mamá gasped. "Is there an antidote?"

"There might be if it is what I think it is, but it's going to cost you a good copper." The doctor closed the cork and got out of his seat. He wrote on a pad of paper. "This is the price. Do you think you can come up with that sum?"

Mamá held the note in her hand, tears spilling down her cheeks.

"We'll see what we can do," Papá said from the doorway.

That night, Mamá and Papá left our home with me in charge of Maria, my two other sisters and my baby brother, Leo. When the sun poked through the windows, I held my crying brother and rocked him back and forth like Mamá, but it wasn't enough.

Voices drifted through the walls from outside. The familiar sound of Mamá's voice set off Leo's wailing and thrashing until I could barely hold him. Mamá smashed through the front door, skipping Leo and me, and ran into my bedroom where Maria lay.

Papá stood at the front gate, holding out a sack of coins to a man I'd never seen before. "Take it. We'll pay you the rest soon."

The man had a top hat, a smart black jacket, and a gold chain hanging from his pocket. He wrinkled his nose at Papá as if he were a rat. "I'll only sell you half the serum. These things aren't free, you know."

Mamá's sharp wail cut across our wooden house. "No! No! Maria! No. Not my Maria."

This couldn't be good.

Papá bolted through the front door as I wrestled to keep hold of Baby Leo. If Mamá's sob crushed my hope, Papá's deep bellows broke my spirit. I set Leo in his crib and inched toward the door. Hot tears gathered at the corners of my eyes, but I sniffed them back in. This had to be some terrible nightmare. Little girls didn't die. I hadn't died from drinking from Lady Arabella's bottle. When I crossed into the room, I stopped at the door.

Mamá held a limp Maria to her chest. "No. My daughter. No. We needed the antidote sooner."

Papá's face reddened with grief and tears and twisted lines.

Maria was gone.

That was how I found out I was blessed with immunity to poison.

Lady Arabella paid off my parents with clothes and scholarships for each of us children to attend the most prestigious schools in all of Aetherfall, but it would never bring back Mamá's joy or Maria.

I promised myself that day that I would never let the lack of money destroy my life again.

Chapter One

Camilla

Eleven Years Later

The invitation materialized from thin air again. My hands trembled with the thick paper between my fingers and thumbs, solid and real. Though my eyes scanned the elegant penmanship, I only read the last words: ONE MUST WIN.

My heartbeat thundered in my ears. I ripped the parchment into a pile of confetti. The shreds fell onto the counter like evidence of a mad eighteen-year-old girl who couldn't control her panic.

The small apothecary waiting room around me witnessed my lunacy. One old lady watched from her seat two yards away. She furrowed her eyebrows behind thick spectacles, and an older gentleman sat across from her, snoring with his head tilted far to the side and his mouth hanging open.

The humble room reminded me that this was the life I'd chosen. My dream to become a rich man's wife had crashed and burned like Sky Manor when it had fallen into the Aether Sea. This apothecary job provided for my needs and my family's, so I should be glad my boss hadn't bought an automaton to do my work. My fingers brushed against the rough brown fabric of the dress I had bought myself, and I cringed.

Only six months ago, I wouldn't have been caught dead in anything that wasn't petal soft and coated with the finest perfumes.

But even so, I wouldn't succumb to the lure of this invitation.

I scooped the pieces of paper that had fallen on my work counter into a waste basket.

Never again would I sink so low as to play a game with my life for something as trivial as money—though silver might speed up my beau's proposal and clothe me in something more fashionable.

No, in the previous Sky Manor game, I'd learned my lesson. Money had never made me happy, dating the richest fellow in school had poisoned my soul, and I'd almost lost the one I loved over riches.

The bell hanging above the door jingled.

I straightened my posture to welcome the person coming into the shop, but it wasn't a customer. Our clients didn't wear fine gray jackets and gold cufflinks.

Wes Acton smirked at me from the entrance as the door shut. His blue eyes smiled, but a mocking twinkle twitched at the corner of his mouth. "Camilla Carranza, is that you?"

Cheeks ablaze and heart skittering, I managed to stretch my lips into a placid smile and tamed the part of me that wanted the wood timber beneath my boots to swallow me whole. "Good to see you, too. How can I help?"

He crossed the several paces to the counter, grimacing at the sleeping man and tipping his hat to the scowling elderly woman.

A chuckle burbled from my throat at how the woman narrowed her gray eyes at him.

Then, Wes blocked my view of the woman. His ravishing face still could lure me to appreciate his finer features, and it pinched at a nerve in my neck. He had the *blessing* to sway people without much effort. "You know I haven't a need for such medicines."

"Why are you here?"

"Because I have an invitation for you."

"I'm not much obliged to accept any invitations these days."

"You're a beautiful young lady. I'm sure you know that. It's been too long since we've seen you at a societal ball." He glanced down over my body. "If you're worried about the dress, I can help."

I rolled my eyes. "Stop with your flattery. What do you want, and how did you know to find me here?"

"You do cut to business. I always liked that about you."

I crossed my arms, covering myself so he'd lift his eye from my curves.

"If you hadn't been Ben's girl, I would have taken you for myself."

"And who says I would have been willing to court you?"

His cheeks tipped up to one side. "It's no secret that you were pursuing a beau who had coin to spare."

"What do you want?" My tone could cut through metal.

"The Aetherfall Elite wanted to extend an invitation to you." He produced a missive with a red wax seal with three torches on it.

"I don't want it. Keep your invitation. The answer is no."

Instead of leaving, Wes leaned on the counter with his palms pressed on the wooden top. Fellows like Wes weren't accustomed to hearing no for an answer. "Camilla, I know you were on scholarship at prep school and that you work here to pay your family's many debts."

"Then, your investigations should also have told you that I am not interested in anything you have to offer."

He leaned closer, too close, but I refused to back away from someone who enjoyed lording his power over the less fortunate.

His next words came out in a whisper. "Then sell me a batch of your special medicine."

I pressed my fingernails into my arms to tame the trembling. "I don't know what you mean."

Wes drew so close I could smell his minty breath. "Show up to my manor after work. I promise Aetherfall Elite thinks you'd make an excellent candidate. What do you have to lose? You might even find yourself another rich beau."

"I'm not available."

"We all heard that you're with Rupert now. Poor scoundrel, he hasn't proposed yet, has he?"

The question stabbed like a knife to the gut.

"I didn't think so. I'll leave the invite on the counter for you to consider." He strode out the door, bell jingling in his wake.

Another invitation? The creepy one that arrived like a ghost each week was bad enough. This one lay in front of me, tiny and real. For most of my time in prep school, I'd longed for the Aetherfall Elite to give me this, but now that school was over and Ben, my imprisoned ex-boyfriend, wasn't vying for me, I'd gotten what I'd always wanted.

This invitation meant I'd forever be invited to societal balls where the most lucrative business dealings were made. Rupert might even be able to come with me; he was a Nelson, after all—shunned but from a wealthy bloodline. And if he formed a good business transaction, he might even propose.

The door jingled again.

CHAPTER TWO

Rupert

TONIGHT WAS THE NIGHT. No more waiting, no more second-guessing. I was finally going to propose to the girl I loved—and tell her she didn't have to worry about money anymore because of my unexpected inheritance.

I adjusted the cravat at my neck for the fifth time. Did I look all right? Was this good enough for a proposal? I checked my reflection in a shop window, patted down some hair that had started to stick up at the back, then strolled down the street at a brisk pace. Dusk was falling; soon, the only outdoor light would be from the metal lampposts positioned around the city of Aetherfall like golems. Camilla's shift would end before I arrived if I didn't hurry up.

I'd been carrying this ring in my pocket for months now, dying to tell her I was ready to move forward in our relationship, but I'd wanted to make sure things would be different this time. I'd given my heart to her before, only for her to turn around and stab me in the back when she'd left me for my rich cousin. I wasn't going to let myself be fooled twice, no matter how much I adored her.

That was why I'd hired Zenith, a former assassin-turned-ally I'd gotten to know a few months ago when we'd both made the mistake of accepting an invitation to Sky Manor. Though he wasn't doing criminal work anymore—as far as I knew—his skillset made him the ideal candidate to watch Camilla for suspicious behavior.

But he hadn't had anything to report. Since our time at Sky Manor, Camilla had worked hard not to be the person she once was, the kind who'd stooped to brewing poisons for the sake of money. She'd sworn she was done with that life, that she wanted to live honestly from now on—like I did.

If only she knew how much it had pained me to hear her say that. She still didn't know about my past, not really. I'd cleaned up my act when I'd met her, saying goodbye to a rather lucrative smuggling operation I'd kept going for almost five years. If anyone at the academy had wanted something snuck in or out, whether it was alcohol, money, or even people—I'd been the one they turned to. Only my old friend Jessie knew the full story, and I trusted her to take my secret to her grave.

I crossed a busy intersection, nearly colliding with a careless cyclist when he turned the corner. He spewed a few curses as he wobbled past, but I ignored him. Nothing could dampen my spirits tonight.

Until I spotted Wes Acton slinking into the apothecary where Camilla worked.

Just the sight of that creep made my blood boil. He was one of my cousin's rich friends from the academy. I'd had more than a few bad run-ins with him over the years. He and my cousin Ben had relished tormenting me for being the son of the Nelson family maid, beating me senseless anytime they felt like it. And Wes's ability to charm others had been particularly useful when they'd needed a teacher to turn a blind eye to their abuse, leaving me with more bruises and broken bones than any kid should endure.

When we'd graduated a few months ago, I'd hoped that would be the last time I ever saw him. It seemed luck wasn't on my side. What was he doing here?

I peeked in one of the windows, stomach dropping at the sight of him looming over Camilla at the counter. His face was far too close to hers, so why wasn't she backing away?

A memory of her hanging all over Ben's arm sprang to the forefront of my mind. When I'd lost my money in a card game last year, she'd dropped me faster than I could blink. Was it happening again? Was she about to leave me for Wes?

My chest went tight, and I stumbled away from the window. A few moments later, the door chimed, and Wes appeared in all his patrician glory. I ducked into the shadows of the nearby alley, then poked my head around. Wes turned up his jacket collar before sauntering off like a gambler who'd just been dealt the winning hand.

"Hey, Wes!" I called, stepping back onto the main road. My hand trembled at my side; in all our time at the academy, I'd never once sought him out. I'd done everything I could to avoid him and Ben, even to the point of hiding in a broom closet once.

But that was before I'd survived a deadly manor intent on turning me into the worst version of myself. A school bully wasn't anywhere near as frightening as that.

Wes spun around with a curious glint in his eye, but it hardened when his gaze landed on me. His lips spread into a wolfish grin. "Rupert, is that you?"

I smothered the instinct to run as he ambled over. "What were you doing with Camilla?" There was no point in wasting time with pleasantries when speaking to Wes was anything but pleasant.

Wes chuckled as he stuck a hand in his pocket. "Just catching up. I wanted to make sure she was doing all right after everything. A girl like that is used to certain niceties. Boggles my mind that she went from Ben back to . . ." He wrinkled his nose at my suit, which was admittedly a bit worn. "But perhaps Camilla will change her mind yet. She's good at that, isn't she?"

I gritted my teeth, fire licking at my chest. "She's mine, Wes. If you know what's good for you, you'll stay away from her."

Wes raised his eyebrows. "Ooh, that's new. A little more swagger in your step after stealing her back from your cousin, eh?" The humor drained from his face as he stepped closer and jabbed me in the chest. "Listen, scum. Ben may be out of the picture now, but that doesn't mean you get to pretend you're anything more than a dog. Go back to trembling with your tail between your legs, or you'll regret it."

I swallowed, head instinctively nodding before I could stop myself. Every bit the scared dog he claimed I was. I thought I'd gotten rid of my yellow streak at Sky Manor, but it seemed I was just as much of a coward as ever.

"Good," Wes sneered, then strolled down the road like he hadn't a care in the world.

A stray thought entered my brain before I turned and went into the apothecary: How much would Zenith charge if I asked him to get rid of that fool?

Chapter Three

Camilla

Rupert strode toward me in his roughspun jacket and plaid pants. My breath caught. Even Wes with his ability to sway hearts had nothing on Rupert. A month ago, I'd had no idea how Rupert found out about my decision to work here, but he had, and I wouldn't trade these evenings with him for all the world. My heart danced with excitement each day when he picked me up from this job to walk me across town to my crammed house in the Yellow District. But today, my stomach twisted into anxious knots.

I untied the apron around my waist and waved at the apothecary in the back room.

"See you next week, Camilla," the apothecary shouted.

Rupert lifted his dark eyebrows into an arch that told me he was excited to see me again. I passed a looking glass and caught the stupid smile that crept along my mouth. My expression couldn't be helped. I scooped up the invitation on the counter and dragged Rupert out of the front door. We had a ball to attend tomorrow night.

The bell jingled as Rupert shut the apothecary door behind us. Clomping metallic hooves, whirring cogs, and humming voices on the street filled my ears. I fitted my arm into his elbow and attempted to calm the pounding in my chest. Rupert was no fool. I had to find the perfect concoction of words to convince him that this function would change our lives for the better.

Though those were my thoughts, I shoved the paper into his grasp. "We should attend."

"Have you read the invitation?" Rupert held the parchment in his hands and glanced toward the road at passing pedestrians so as not to bump into them.

"No, but Wes Acton delivered it himself." I clung to Rupert's arm.

Carriages clunked by on the brick road. Merchants called from their shops to attract the crowd of workers heading home for the night. The crowded mass of downtrodden people chiseled a hole in my heart. I could never be satisfied with this life.

"You should read it yourself." Rupert passed the elegant missive back to me.

All appeared as expected. Elegant penmanship. The word "exclusive" was used twice. *Bring your special brew with you and dress in formal attire.*

I flicked a look at Rupert.

He met my stare with one eyebrow raised, silently asking the question he hadn't given voice to in the past six months. *Have you stopped making poisons?*

At Sky Manor, I'd promised to quit poisoning. And I had.

With jerky movements, I folded the paper and stuffed it into the pocket of my dress.

The city's bustle filled the silence of our dropped conversation. I clung tightly to Rupert's rough jacket, and he led us across the street to a small park with benches and a tiny pond in the center.

Though nature couldn't completely muffle the noise on the streets, it did a decent job giving my ears a reprieve. My mind, on the other hand, shouted at me. *Rupert won't like this. You'll break your vow, and then what will that make you? A murderer.*

Gnats swarmed across my vision, and I swatted them. If only I could swat away this yearning for more. Rupert stopped at a bench with a very pretty view of the pond. Tall grass lined each side of us, and red sunlight reflected off the water.

"Please, sit with me." Rupert gestured and held out my hand as if I were delicate glass. "We've needed to have a serious conversation."

Is this it? Is he going to propose? If that is the case, he must have made enough income to support a family. Then we'll have no need for Wes Acton's silly games. The gallop of my heart did not match my slow movements as I sat on the bench.

Resisting the urge to bite my lip, I watched him work his jaw and fiddle with something in his pocket. The shape of a box of some sort took form beneath the cloth.

I inhaled a steadying breath. The answer to his question appeared on the tip of my tongue like the sweetest flavored peach I'd ever eaten.

Yes, you fool, just state your question. Yes, I'll marry you. Even my thoughts had a desperate tone, which didn't suit someone like me, but it couldn't be helped. Tears warmed the corners of my eyes until they were ready to burst.

Rupert flipped out the tail of his jacket and sat a foot away from me with a seriousness in his dark brown eyes; those two soulful moons drank in the sight of me and seemed to see beyond my exterior person.

"Camilla, as you know, we've had many highs and lows." His smooth voice had the perfect masculine pitch, though I wanted to speed up his speech.

"Yes, Rupert." I folded my hands together over my lap, attempting a poised position.

"At Sky Manor, I'd nearly lost all hope of us ever courting again."

I swallowed a lump in my throat, full of guilt over having chosen to court Rupert's cousin, Ben, because of coin and the deadly touch he'd wielded. My immunity to poison, coupled with Ben's poison touch, had made us seem like a match from above.

"Since then, I—I . . ." His mouth parted, forming a syllable that wouldn't quite emerge.

"We've been together, and you'd like to make this more formal?" The suggestion spilled out without my consent, but he was speaking so slow.

"Yes, in many ways." Right when the edges of his mouth lifted to create his full grin, he pressed his lips together, furrowed his eyebrows, and said, "But, Camilla, it scares me that you grew so excited for Wes's invitation."

My heart sank into my gut. This wasn't a proposal. He remained uncertain about where I stood in my desire for funds and in my love for him over money and fame.

"Forgive me, beloved, but I simply do not trust Wes Acton's intentions." He reached for my hands, but I pulled away.

"No, you don't trust me."

"I do trust you."

"Then what is it? Is it that you don't want to start a family with me?"

"No, Camilla, I want to marry you. You are my treasure. I also want you to be satisfied even if I can't provide for your tastes."

"So, it's a matter of position and funds?"

Rupert shook his head.

"Come with me to Wes's Elite meeting. I won't bring my poisons like it suggests, and if they boot us out the doors for that reason, then we'll know for certain they had bad intentions." I scooted closer to Rupert and cupped his cheek to turn him to meet my gaze. "There's nothing wrong with using your connections to better your position."

He placed his warm palm over my hand. An unreadable expression twitched beneath my touch.

"Do you hate all of your cousin's friends so much?" I asked.

He flinched, and I used that as my cue to remove my hand. We hadn't spoken of Ben since the game or that Ben had been imprisoned for murder at Sky Manor.

"They aren't Ben," I said.

"I wouldn't be so sure." He stood and gazed over the lake. "I should take you home now before it gets too dark."

The rest of the walk to my small cottage home was silent. It gave me enough time to ruminate over my throbbing heart and how Rupert might never trust me enough to propose matrimony. Then again, he had also mentioned my love for fine dresses, but that he couldn't provide them for me. Well, he hadn't said that in so many words. That certainly must be what he'd meant.

When we turned the street corner to my home, a tall gangly man with an eighteen-inch top hat exited our gate. The debt collector.

I passed Rupert a rueful smile for having to witness more of my poverty.

He gave a gentle squeeze of my hand. "I'll pick you up on Monday before work?"

Tears threatened to fall, but not the happy type from earlier. I nodded.

Mamá shouted and waved from the porch of our little shack. "Rupert, come join us for supper."

"Thank you, Señora Carranza. I wish to stay, but I must return to do some business." He glanced at me and then waved to Mamá.

"Then, you come over tomorrow. I'll kill a chicken for you." Mamá wasn't asking this time. It was a command. The door shut behind her, leaving us alone before our rickety gate with my sisters peeking through the window at us.

Rupert chuckled. "I love you, Camilla." He squared up to me and held both of my hands in his. "I also know you. Don't go to Wes's ball."

I resisted the urge to scowl at him, keeping each of my facial muscles as still as possible.

He kissed my knuckles and opened my front gate. The hurry in his step gave me pause, but I wouldn't push the issue. I strode around him and through my gate. In a few quick steps, I arrived at my front door and turned to wave at him. He was off, not bothering to wait for me to blow him a kiss like I always did. His behavior smelled of secrets.

Though he'd asked me *not* to attend Wes's ball, I'd never given my word.

And if he failed to disclose his whereabouts, I, too, could have my own indiscretions. *Is that the correct word? Well, I know what I mean.*

Me attending the ball would prove advantageous for Rupert even though he wouldn't be aware of who'd won him that favor.

I crossed into my home, passed my noisy younger sisters, passed Papá, and headed straight for my closet to the selection of gowns Ben had once bought for me. I'd need to do some mending for the next night.

CHAPTER FOUR

Camilla

RUPERT DIDN'T ARRIVE TO eat Mamá's chicken the following night, and he forewent the opportunity to stop me from executing the plan he so detested. I slipped on the expensive gown I'd kept locked at the back of the closet for all these months. The tight corset and heavy dress couldn't be more welcome after all the scratchy material I'd submitted to since I hadn't had a place to wear such finery.

"Don't wait up for me, Mamá." I slipped on a black hood to remain inconspicuous while crossing the city and slid out the front door.

She said something in return, but I didn't give her the chance to interrogate me, knowing she'd forget about her concern in a moment when my not-so-baby brother Leo tore through the house playing the outlaw from Terramor in the Wild West.

The mild night swallowed me in its embrace, taking me to the bowels of society masquerading as the gems. Rupert had a point in not trusting Wes, yet lack of money had a way of keeping people away from their needs and desires. Determined, I set my path to the White District with only clacking automatons doing errands for their masters and my heel taps echoing on the darkened road. A rat scuttled far into the shadows between buildings. Once I crossed under the city bridge, I'd be in the wealthy sector of town where the Aetherfall Elite Ball took place. It was the same location that had nearly lost me my heart two years back.

Two Years Earlier

Lights twinkled, and my cheap dress swayed beneath me. I fitted my arm over Rupert's and placed my hand in his to start our dance. We fit like two puzzle pieces meant to be together.

The music waltzed through the packed room with the Saint Clockwell Preparatory Academy student body twirling about the grand ballroom in perfect synchrony. Yet, I couldn't force a smile to my lips.

Rupert inclined his head close to my ear. "What's wrong?"

I averted my gaze to Rupert's cousin, a tall and stately fellow wearing an outfit that could pay off my family's debt. How could I reprimand Rupert for being born poor? Instead, I heaved a calming breath and pushed through the final steps required of the dancers.

"Camilla, please tell me." Rupert set in place his heart-melting grin that somehow managed to make his eyes glitter in the lamplight.

"You're cute when you're concerned." I hooked my arm through his and walked off the ballroom floor, still keeping tabs on his cousin Ben.

The moment we arrived at the outer rim, I yanked myself free of Rupert and straightened my posture. This wasn't going to be an easy night.

"I'll get you something to drink." His softer edges had shifted into taut lines. I wished to smooth my fingertips over his face so his previous expression would return. Yet I had no choice but to do the opposite.

Someone take my pistol out and shoot me in the heart, I thought to myself. I truly deserved to be taken out for what I was about to do.

A wayward hair slipped from Rupert's hair, gracing his temple. I caged my hand with the other to staunch the impulse to push his hair back in place. He walked off to find me my favorite tea. That was when I marched to the gaming tables where Ben had gone with a group of his equally fortunate friends.

Every step forward brought me closer to keeping my commitment to never being in want, but farther from the one person who knew me and still loved me. I couldn't turn away. A nasty creditor's letter threatened to take my parents' home if they didn't pay up. I'd have to gamble away my heart to keep my sisters and brother safe.

I stood behind the golden-haired Ben, having sensed his perusal many times before. My beauty would have to become my weapon. Ben slipped off his white glove, which I'd never seen him do before. Something about the tint of his eyes darkened as he reached for my dopey classmate Horace. On instinct, I slipped my fingers into Ben's palm.

A warm tingle flowed in wandering waves up my arm and warmed my body. The instant connection stole my breath away. Even Rupert didn't have the uplifting sensation I only got when I worked with poisons. It was almost as if Ben had a poison touch.

Ben's blue eyes popped wide open in shock, letting me know that he felt the same sensation I had. The same swarm of comforting tendrils shot through my blood.

Rupert arrived with his vanilla-and-spice scent like a cloud around him. His eyebrows drew together like a question mark, asking why I stood with his cousin. He'd never believe I'd stoop to trading him in for a wealthier prospect.

"Why don't you join in the game?" I suggested to Rupert.

Ben chuckled. "Why don't you, Rupert? I'd love to see what a poor scoundrel like you can do."

Rupert wouldn't back down from such a challenge, and he lost everything that night.

STEELING MY NERVES WITH the quick roll of my shoulders, I prepared to repair the damage I'd done to Rupert. The fumes in the city air clogged my throat from all the industry that surrounded the districts, but I wouldn't be perturbed—no, that wasn't the word—deterred by anything tonight.

Rupert will feel secure enough in his finances to propose.

I lifted my chin higher and strode with the same snooty strut of all the legitimate students at Saint Clockwell Preparatory who hadn't required a scholarship to attend. The darkness beneath the bridge contrasted with the mansion across the street that had enough gas lamps on the front walkway to brighten my entire neighborhood at night.

Carriages lined the front entrance as guests were delivered to the front steps, where automatons received them and offered metal arms for support. Even from this distance, the women's dresses shimmered from expensive threads and weaving. A shiver of excitement danced up my spine at being able to enjoy such beauty again. But heat filled my cheeks at such a thought. Silver and gold could never satisfy—I'd learned that lesson—but, oh, how they delighted the senses.

Even with my plain cloak, no one gave me a second glance as I marched around the gate and beneath the columns to the main entrance. My confident gait did its job. Later that night, the red dress my ex-boyfriend Ben had bought for me would have to draw the eye, setting me up as a player in this little game the Elite played.

Men in top hats gathered their partners from the coaches. Ladies in feathered hats and decorative cogs chatted about the governor's presence. They slid their glittering masks in place to convert themselves into animals or vacant-eyed mannequins. I hadn't a mask to wear, having sold all of mine to help my family. *If only I'd kept one.*

I sped up and craned my neck at the crowd gathered at the open doors.

"He's here tonight?" a man in a green top hat and a gold mask asked the older woman beside him in a gem-studded blue mask. She held a gold pocket watch with a small hologram image of a man projected three inches above the device.

"So is his son." The woman stretched her neck to peer around the crowd and turned back to the hologram.

Soldiers marched in with pistols strapped to their sides, wearing the red military costumes typical of Aetherfall. The woman snapped the lid of the device shut, and the governor strode toward us, as elegant as ever, with a perverse smile twisting his mustache up at the ends. His son, Horace, trailed behind him.

We'd called Horace "Horsy" at preparatory because of his tuft of mousy hair that never wanted to be tamed. He kept his head down, not bothering to woo the crowds eager for a piece of him. Ben hated Horace more than any other lad at school, and though I now had no connection to Ben, my nose still crinkled at the sight of the lanky classmate who'd liked to stare in my direction during literature classes.

Just as Horace passed in front of me, he lifted his head like he could sense me watching him. I ducked, pretending I had dropped something on the ground. Why had I done that? Perhaps it was the need to focus on the current mission. My old life had been buried with Sky Manor when it crashed and burned in the sea.

The masked couple in front of me headed into the main entrance, as did the dozen other couples who'd stopped to allow the Aetherfall governor easy passage into this gala. I stayed close to the couple ahead of me, trying to seem a part of their group while I scanned the marble floors within Wes's city estate. The silks and lace of the ladies' gowns and the eccentric masks with mechanical flowers and real flowers left me breathless. We shuffled through the atrium, where a butler and automatons took my cape and checked my invitation.

The latest model automaton with polished metal held my invite and said in a robotic voice, "You are an approved guest. Enter." Its humanoid arm gestured to the open doorways behind it.

Upon entering the hall, a giant rectangular room stretched in every direction, with tables all along the edges. The music of stringed instruments crested into a breathtaking melody both painful and sweet. Chandeliers poured yellow light from high above and reflected off the window-lined wall across from me. In a giant empty space at the center, I found Horace chatting with an older woman who had styled her white hair into the shape of a conch.

I dodged to the left, making sure my back faced him as I found a server with a flute of pink liquid. I scooped it between my fingers and kept moving as far away from Horace as I could get. Wes hadn't invited me to this event because he was trying to be nice.

Where is Wes?

The majority of guests wore masks over their eyes, unlike me - leaving me exposed while others could hide.

"Lady Carranza," Wes called from behind me, "I'm so glad you didn't put your mask on yet."

Spinning to meet his gaze, I rolled my shoulders back and tipped my head in a way that Ben had once called flirty.

"Your invitation lured me in."

A smirk tiptoed across his lips. "Come to the back room with me. A few of us are meeting there before the festivities begin."

When he said a few, he meant over a dozen of the most popular and powerful alumni at Saint Clockwell, save Ben—and Arden, who had been murdered.

The cozy little room quieted the moment I entered. A table of card players peered in my direction while the ladies around the small fire smiled behind their hands like they had some secret they weren't sharing. Wes closed the door behind him, drowning out the velvet melody beyond and shutting me in a smaller room with rancid cigarette smoke.Sweat slickened my palms.

"I didn't realize this was a masquerade." I gritted my teeth to keep from sharing that I had sold all my masks to pay my parents' bills last month. I hadn't expected to need them any longer.

The grooves bracketing Wes's grin deepened, and he chuckled. "I believe we have extra masks." He continued to lead me to the lonely back corner.

Something wasn't right about this situation. Maybe it was the sideways glances of people or that my old friends didn't bother to greet me.

"Please take a seat." He gestured to three armchairs facing each other.

The girls across the room began to murmur.

Of course, I widened my lips into a practiced smile as I placed my bum on an armchair cushion that was more expensive than my family's home. Wes took a seat beside me and scooted very close.

Conversations started up again, and the shuffle of cards resumed at the gambling tables. Though they all seemed to gain a sense of normalcy, I couldn't quite shrug off the apprehension that had appeared when I'd entered the room.

"Did you bring your brew?" His sharp blue eyes shone with hunger. Whatever he planned couldn't be good.

"I don't deal in poisons anymore."

His smile faltered, but he recovered by leaning in closer. "Then what are you doing here?"

"You didn't specify what you wanted exactly, so even if I did still use my skill, I couldn't have helped you."

"I know you believe yourself free from accusation, but Arden's body was found before Sky Manor sank into the ocean. A coroner did get a chance to examine it, and then there is the matter of video footage. You don't exactly come across as innocent."

I squinted at him. "What are you getting at?" My fingers pressed harder into the glass flute.

"His fingernails had evidence of being poisoned." Wes drew nearer now. So close, he whisked a curl off my shoulder. "Ben cannot be exonerated because of the films and the pressure from the press, but what if we could retrieve films from the dinner party when you passed him a shiny object under the table, and what if the coroner had new testimony come to light?"

My mouth dried with his insinuation. The panic in my chest knocked so hard it might break a rib. "I'm not the only one who could have given him that brew. You still lack evidence."

"The testimony of Saint Clockwell's finest should count for something." He gestured to the others, who now seemed wrapped up in conversations and games.

"This hardly seems like an invitation."

"You're right. It isn't. We have a problem that you can solve while keeping us all away from the constable's eye."

"You still have no real evidence to accuse me." I stood, ready to storm out of the room and leave the mansion. The unease slithering through my gut began to throb.

Wes grabbed my wrist and yanked me down. "You're not understanding. I have a favor to ask, and in return, I will make a few calls for you . . . and Rupert."

I stilled, listening.

"Rupert needs a favor." His cheek twitched with some emotion I couldn't decipher. "He keeps secrets from you, Camilla, and you want position."

A huff of breath rushed between my teeth. Did he take me for a fool? If I gave in to his so-called deal, then he would never stop using me. This wasn't an invitation to be like the others in the group.

Wes gestured toward the rest of the room. "You can be one of us where the important business in Aetherfall transpires. You went to many backrooms like this when Ben was around, so you understand the many benefits." His fingers gripped my wrist like a vice.

Ripping from his hold, I adjusted my dress and rolled my shoulders back with a confidence I didn't possess. He was telling the truth about how prestige was gained in this city, and Rupert didn't have the wealth to circumvent the connections required to succeed in his new business ventures. Perhaps I should consider this proposition.

"Now, you know our organization requires an initiation. Here's your test." Wes leaned up to my ear as if to share a secret. "I need you to kill the governor's son tonight."

My bottom lip quivered.

He continued, "Horace will inherit his dad's position, and he's an unruly sort. He doesn't understand what's expected. I thought your poison would be the easiest route for you to achieve our goal."

This was wrong. This was the opposite of what I wanted. I could never do that, even to someone like Horace.

Though my thoughts raged at me, I said in my calmest tone, "And if I don't?"

Wes let out a chuckle. "Then someone else will do the job and you might have an accident or a constable at your door. I can't decide which one I like better. Of course, you are a pretty thing. It would be a shame to waste so much beauty. Ben hasn't a companion in his cell. He might enjoy your company."

The knocking in my chest intensified. He wasn't giving me a choice in the matter. And if that was the case, I had to find a way to save Horace and myself. I pulled away from Wes and shifted my features into the expression I used when I flirted. "Wes Acton, how long do I have to achieve your goal in order for you to accept me into the Elite?"

"You have twelve hours, my dear. I expect no evidence and for you to show up to my bedroom in the morning with the good news."

"And how am I to know which of these many rooms is yours?"

"I'll inform the servants that a beautiful lady with tan skin and the face of a goddess will be seeking me out. They'll be enthralled by my conquest."

I gagged but hid it with a fake laugh. "My mask?"

Wes snapped his fingers at a lady playing cards to get her attention. "Give me Lady Camilla's mask."

The girl in a fluffy dress with a tower of blonde hair smirked. "Just as you requested." She pulled out a box with the most gorgeous mask I'd ever seen. Sparkling crystals encircled the eyeholes, blood red gems wove in beautiful patterns around the lacy ironwork, and black velvet covered the rest of the space, giving it a regal yet mysterious feel. It was so like the one Lady Arabella had chosen that dreaded day when I'd stolen her vial as a child. I bit down on my trembling lip to prevent a gasp from escaping.

"Here you go." Wes placed the mask over my face and began to tie it. The gentle pressure of his hands sent shivers of disgust vibrating through my midsection. He fastened the strips with jerky motions and tapped my shoulder.

"See you in the morning."

I jolted to my feet, needing to hear no more of Wes's poisonous words. My heels tapped across the floor, and my vision blurred at the edges. What foolishness had led me to believe the Elite would ever truly accept me?

Rupert had been right about not going to this elegant affair. Now, I had until morning to hold back the tides of murder while trying to save myself from certain doom.

Chapter Five

Rupert

Earlier That Evening

"I'd sooner catch that man's shadow than him, it seems," I muttered to myself as I wandered through the city. I'd been searching for Zenith for the past several hours, but since I had no idea where he lived—and neither Jessie nor Maple had seen him today—I was running out of places to look.

He'd always been the one to come to me, which I hadn't realized until now put me at a distinct disadvantage. I was just about to give up when a voice emerged from the dark alley I was passing.

"I heard you were looking for me."

I yelped and nearly jumped out my skin as Zenith materialized at my side. How had I not noticed him? He wasn't exactly a short man, though I supposed his black cloak was a great help in camouflaging his willowy form.

I coughed to hide my embarrassment. "Zenith, what impeccable timing. I need your help."

The ex-assassin fell into step beside me as we meandered down the street. His expression was guarded, giving no indication whether he was glad to help or irritated at my request.

"Is this about Camilla?"

"Sort of," I admitted. "What do you know about Wes Acton?"

Zenith didn't answer for a long moment, as he was prone to do, and the only sounds were our footfalls on the cobbled sidewalk. We passed a few stores with various trinkets gleaming from the shop windows.

"He's among the wealthiest gentlemen in the city, and his family hosts the Aetherfall Elite Ball every summer. Never had any personal dealings with him."

"Have you heard if he or anyone else in his Elite group is involved in anything . . . shady?"

"Define 'shady.'" His deadpan tone made it impossible to tell if he was trying to be humorous.

"Anything I wouldn't want Camilla to be part of." That definition encompassed plenty, and it told him why this was so important to me.

"Ah. In that case, yes."

I grimaced. "That's what I was afraid you were going to say." I rubbed the back of my neck. "Wes Acton personally invited her to the ball yesterday, and she was really wanting to go. . . . Guess I was right to ask her not to."

Zenith hummed in his throat, the sound neither supportive nor critical.

"You don't think she'll listen, do you?"

The man pursed his lips, considering my question. "I think Camilla loves you, but until she knows the truth about the fortune you've come into, she's going to keep looking for ways to secure your future. Whatever that may look like."

"You're wrong," I said sharply. "Camilla promised she wasn't going to go back to her old ways, and in all the time you've been spying on her, hasn't she proven that?"

Zenith's eyes flashed with annoyance. "If you're so confident in your girlfriend, then why haven't you asked me to stop following her?"

His inquiry stopped me in my tracks. I couldn't deny the truth of it, no matter how much I wished otherwise. I didn't trust her. Not yet.

"Soon," I promised. "Soon, I'll be sure, and then you can go back to doing whatever else it is you do."

When he didn't respond, I turned, wondering if he didn't believe me, but Zenith had disappeared. Again.

I groaned. How did he *do* that?

I tramped through the streets without much thought or care where I ended up. I didn't want to distrust Camilla, but wasn't it only fair after what she'd done? Maybe I was being unreasonable. It *had* been ten months, after all. And just yesterday I'd been so set on proposing, only to pull back at the first sign of trouble. But Camilla hadn't hidden the invitation from Wes; she'd even let me read it first.

I looked up, finding myself in front of her family's cottage. Seemed my heart had taken the reins instead of my head tonight. I checked my watch, realizing with a guilty twinge that I'd missed dinner. I hoped Mrs. Carranza wasn't upset.

I squared my shoulders and rapped on the door, an apology already forming in my throat.

Camilla's mother, a short woman with sad eyes, opened the door. Her expression brightened upon seeing me, but then her eyebrows pinched together. "Rupert, is something wrong?" She glanced behind me. "Where's Camilla?"

My heart skipped a beat. "What do you mean? She's not here?"

Mrs. Carranza shook her head. "I thought she was meeting you? She was all dressed up like she was going somewhere special."

"But I thought we were having dinner here tonight. Where would—" I broke off as understanding hit me. If Camilla had gone out, there was only one place she could be: that infernal ball. It was tonight, wasn't it?

I hid the grimace twitching at my lips and quickly lied that I'd forgotten we'd made arrangements yesterday. "What time did she leave?"

Mrs. Carranza didn't seem completely convinced by my excuse, but she didn't comment on it. "About fifteen minutes ago."

"Thank you." I tipped my hat and strode off, ready to break down the doors of Wes's estate if I had to.

It didn't take long to find the mansion. Even though I'd never been to this part of the city before, the long line of coaches made it easy to pick out. It seemed everyone who was anyone had come tonight. Several photographers were snapping photos as people exited their coaches, though the guests' faces were obscured by sparkling masks in this sea of silk, satin, lace, and feathers. This was the kind of social scene I typically avoided like the plague, whereas Camilla thrived at gatherings like this.

I glanced down at my old suit, all my bluster fading away in the wind. In no way did I look like I belonged here. But I wasn't coming to enjoy the party; I just wanted to get Camilla and get out. Surely they'd let me do that?

But when my turn came to enter, an automaton blocked me with a long mechanical arm. It was a tall, gangly thing with large emerald eyes and antennae on its head that made it look like a metal dragonfly.

"You are not an approved guest. I must ask you to exit the premises immediately."

"You don't understand. I'm just here to find someone. I'm not here for the ball. Let me pass, and I'll be back out within a few minutes."

"I cannot do that," the automaton's dead voice replied. The ends of its antennae began to light up. Was it sending a message to someone inside?

I ran a hand through my hair and took a deep breath, trying not to let my growing anxiety show. "Then could you go find Camilla Carranza and let her know that I'm here? My name is Rupert Nelson."

"I cannot leave this post. Please exit the premises, or I will be forced to remove you."

"But—"

"You heard him, man. Just move already," shouted an angry gentleman a few spots behind me. He waved his gloved hand dismissively. "Some of us actually have invitations to be here."

I spun around to give the man a piece of my mind when a thought struck me. Wouldn't it be easier to find out what Camilla was up to if she didn't know I was here? All I needed was a fancy suit, a mask, and a way to sneak inside. I hurried off to the nearest tailor, who wrinkled his nose at me until I showed him my full coin purse. In a jiffy, I looked like one of the Elite, complete with a green patterned vest and coat uncomfortably similar to my cousin Ben's.

I narrowed my eyes at the dashing gentleman in the full-length mirror. "Maybe something a bit more subtle?" I suggested to the tailor. "It's a masquerade, and I'd like my girlfriend to be surprised when I take off my mask."

The mousy man complained under his breath but scurried off to find something more in line with my tastes. While I waited, I inspected a mannequin with creepy blue eyes that I suspected held a hidden camera. The tailor returned a few minutes later with a long black cloak and an iron mask.

"Will this do?"

I ran my hand along the cloak's smooth fabric, then threw it over my clothes. The material hung almost to the floor, hiding everything but my glossy black boots. The mask was rather monstrous, but it covered my face so well that I hardly recognized myself. "Yes, this will do quite nicely."

It was time to take a page out of Zenith's book. It was time to become invisible.

Chapter Six

Camilla

I'D NEVER HATED ATTENDING a gala more than today. Dresses of wool, purple dyes, extravagant head pieces, and jewels that sparkled under the yellow chandelier light blurred along the edges of my vision. My instinct was to drink in the beautiful sights, but the person at the center of my focus was a classmate I'd teased mercilessly. *Horace Ambrose.*

He stood among a crowd of elders, laughing in a goofy way that crinkled the skin below his eyes and set a shallow indent along both his cheeks. He wasn't exactly ugly, but I'd never call him handsome. I turned to a table with honey tea and glimpsed myself in a decorative mirror. My mask rested atop my nose and high cheeks perfectly, adding a mysterious aura about me. The only evidence of nerves trembled along my full bottom lip. I poured myself a cup, buying myself time to think of a plan.

Wes exited the backroom with a black mask that cut diagonally across his nose and cheeks. "I look forward to our reunion." His teasing tone sharpened a spear of anger through my chest.

My nose flared, and the cool glass in my hand had never felt like a better launching tool. "See you later," I managed to grit out from between my teeth.

The jovial step in Wes's gait had the markings of a schoolboy with a hidden candy in his pocket. I could feel the pressure of my pistol along my thigh, strapped in place where I always kept it. Though I might have quit my poisoning ways, I wasn't about to go without protection in a city where criminals led the masses—I knew that more today than ever.

I can do this. I can come up with a way to save Horace and pretend this night never happened. Wes couldn't possibly have evidence against me. Yet even while repeating the thoughts to myself, I scrambled to come up with a solution to free myself from the Elite's control.

Who could help me? Not Rupert. I gulped the cool tea, tasting the sweet herbs as they sloshed down my throat and burned in my stomach.

The other contestants from Sky Manor—well, besides Arden and Ben—could be of some service. But I suspected that Maple wouldn't be at her bakery at this time of night. She'd know how to handle Wes with her fighting ability. Perhaps she could find someone for me to hire so I could send Wes a message he wouldn't soon forget.

"Excuse me," a male voice said behind me.

I spun around to find a tall man with a square jaw, a simple black mask, and touchable curls.

"Would you join me for a dance?" He extended a white-gloved hand, which reminded me too much of Ben, but his other hand glimmered with the sheen of metal. "I noticed you upon arrival and find you to be the loveliest lady I've met. Do you mind cyborg arms? It doesn't limit my dancing much." His mechanical fingers clicked and churned as he displayed twiddling mechanical appendages.

Inwardly, I groaned at his guilt trip, but outwardly, I set my glass cup on the table and let the edges of my mouth tip up a fraction.

"I'm obliged," I said. No one could accuse me of prejudice against cyborg humans.

He offered his elbow, and we paraded to the dance floor while my thoughts grappled for ways to approach Horace: *Hi, there. I know I was a complete beast to you in school, but let's be friends. Oh, and the Elite want me to murder you, so can you play dead while I figure out a way to flee.*

The man turned to face me and set himself in the expected dance position. I fitted myself into his arms and craned my neck to catch sight of Horace trying to fasten a plain black mask but failing as he spoke to an elegant older woman not twenty feet away. The woman was turned away from me, but something about her erect posture and decadent style of dress kept me looking.

Orchestra music echoed through the hall with the lovely twine of notes mingling together in the most perfect melody. My feet were off dancing before I registered what my body was doing.

"What is your name?" my dance partner asked.

Cringing at him for wanting to engage in small talk, I turned my focus from Horace to whomever guided me through the prescribed steps. I should be kind. "Camilla. And yours?"

"Dunstan. Dunstan Davenport of the *Daily Pen*." He spoke his title like a badge of honor.

"Oh my." I played to his vanity. I supposed that most souls in this room, including myself, wanted to feel famous.

"Yes, we are so excited for what's coming to this city."

"And what is that?"

He leaned closer as if to tell a secret. "The Games." A glimmer of delight shifted behind his eyeholes.

"Didn't Sky Manor crash and burn in the sea?" I managed to keep my voice steady, though I wanted to slap him for his lopsided grin while speaking of something so foul.

"Ahh, my dear, the host of the Game still believes in his cause. The money the Games bring to the city is astronomical. From the four corners, people travel to see the deadly mansion and catch a glimpse of the contestants while they play."

"But there is no mansion." Disgust rolled off my tongue, and I wasn't about to hide it.

"I see this disturbs you. Perhaps you believe yourself superior to the rest of us, not a slave to your coin purse." He lifted my arm, and I spun as required.

When I squared up into his embrace, I roiled with revulsion at his accusation. Riches did run Aetherfall and had been my sole desire since I'd heard Mamá cry over my sister's dead body. A plethora of coin could have prevented me from stealing the poison from Lady Arabella's purse in the first place, but after participating in the sickening game that Dunstan wanted reestablished, I loathed my old ambitions.

"Come on, Camilla, don't think I don't recognize you." A mocking tone coated each word. "Your face covered every newspaper from Aetherfall to Newport."

He'd known who I was. The realization shook me to my core. My body stopped as if my feet had suddenly become blocks of iron bolted to the ground. Dunstan's hand still pushed and tugged into the next dance moves, which caused my body to trip over itself.

Dunstan caught me before I fell and leaned closer to my ear. His cinnamon-and-honey breath curled my already-turbulent emotions, producing a dry heave I could barely hold back. "The host of Sky Manor needs you to return for another scavenger hunt. The heart of the manor won't accept any new contestants until someone has won the last game."

"Let go of me." I pushed against his body, repelling him with all my might.

"You will be even more famous. Every newspaper would love to post your face beneath the headline." He set me upright but kept closer than necessary. "If you could convince Rupert and your other friends to return, the maker of the games would handsomely reward you for your efforts."

"I don't have time for this." I twisted out of his embrace without decorum or care about his good opinion. My hand slipped into the pocket I'd made for all my dresses. The cool metal of my pistol's handle brought me comfort when the rest of the world spun out of control.

Dunstan grabbed my waist and spun me into his body, where we collided in an uncomfortably close position. On instinct, I pulled out my pistol, nuzzled the tip to just below his ribs, and blocked my indiscretion with my position.

"Mr. Dunstan, I've considered your offer, and I feel I must decline. Now, you must stop your pursuits and find a different damsel to hustle." I slipped my pistol back into its confines and strode away with blood pounding through each vein.

I was glancing around at the distracted guests all conversing in tight circles or still dancing with partners when a slow clap met my ears. Wes stood off to the side in his black mask that did nothing to hide the twist of his lips and the laugh lines deeply embedded into his cheeks.

"Tick tock," he said. "Tick tock. You always give the best video footage."

Only eleven hours remained until the Elite would make a formal accusation of murder or I'd show up at Wes's room, confirming that Horace was gone. I should just run away, but where would I go? I couldn't leave my family when they relied on me to pay bills, and I could never leave without Rupert.

No, I'd have to stride right up to Horace and tell him the truth.

Where was he?

Chapter Seven

Rupert

I DIDN'T BOTHER TRYING to get back in through the front entrance this time and instead slunk around to the back of the estate. The only door I could find was locked tight, so I stepped back and eyed the surrounding walls. They weren't *that* tall. Perhaps I could climb over one if I got a running start.

My head swiveled around to make sure there were no cameras or potential witnesses, then I charged toward the wall and jumped, hands stretching upward.

"Agh!" My nose slammed into limestone, and I fell to the ground in a heap of black fabric. I threw the cloak off my face and scowled at the unyielding wall before me.

A bit taller than I'd thought. What would Zenith do if he were here? Certainly not give up.

He wouldn't have made such a fool of himself either. Scaling a wall was child's play for him.

I rubbed my aching nose and took a deep breath. There had to be another way in.

A yew tree stood a few feet away, its thick, twisted limbs reaching for the sky. The sight of it evoked memories of climbing trees as a child, back when the only things one had to worry about were making sure you were home in time for dinner. But I hadn't done anything like that in years. Was it even a viable option?

My eyes trailed upward. The tree's top branches easily surpassed the mansion walls, though they were much narrower than the ones near the base. Still, they should be sturdy enough for my purposes. And once I was up there, I'd be able to get over the wall and drop into the grass.

I glanced down at my new clothes, already regretting this.

Several bruises and scratches later, I was poised atop the yew tree, peering at the unsuspecting revelers like an owl eying a group of mice. Several ladies and gentlemen were ambling about the grounds with glasses in hand, laughing and chatting with ease. None even glanced my way.

I wasn't the praying sort, but I sent up a quick request not to break my neck before I left the safety of the tree. I landed in the grass with a great whoosh and teetered over onto my side. I didn't move, instead doing my best to stifle a cry while I waited for the pain in my feet and ankles to subside. Not exactly the soft landing I'd hoped for, but at least I'd made it.

"Did you hear something?" a feminine voice asked.

I rolled back onto my feet and darted behind a tall bush. My cloak snagged on some leaves, causing a loud rustle when I pulled it away.

"I did that time," replied a man. "It sounds like it's coming from over there near the wall."

"Is that a person back there?"

Blast. I adjusted my hood and mask, then stole across the grounds, ignoring a high-pitched scream in my wake. I just had to find Camilla and get her out of here. No one would recognize me dressed like this, so what did it matter if someone spotted me? All they'd see was a masked figure in a cloak. If I was very unlucky, I might wind up in the newspaper, but it wasn't like anyone would suspect Rupert Nelson, the poor son of a shopkeeper, of trespassing at an event like this.

I ducked inside the mansion, then handed my cloak to an automaton collecting outerwear and did my best to blend in. It was surprisingly easy when everyone was dressed in similar fashion and focused on their own affairs. Several gentlemen conversed in small groups while others swayed with their partners on the dance floor. They moved out of my way as I passed, treating me as politely as if I were the governor himself. Some of the women smiled and waved their fans coquettishly when they saw me, and a server carrying a tray offered me a glass of champagne.

I took the proffered drink and downed it all in one shot, hoping it would chase away the rush of anger in my blood. These people put on such airs. They acted like they were so removed from the common folk, yet all it had taken was a halfway decent disguise and a tree to infiltrate their gathering.

Now, where was Camilla? My eyes swept the ballroom for a tan, dark-haired beauty.

Someone bumped into me. "I'm sorry, sir," mumbled a petite young woman with blue eyes a size too large for her seaweed-green mask. Her aqua dress was covered in folds made to resemble ocean waves, and small white shells adorned both sides of her head.

"Not at all, miss." I smiled to show I'd taken no offense before I remembered she couldn't see my expression. Then something struck me. I knew this girl. "Miss Woodhouse?"

The brown-haired woman scrutinized me, then frowned and shook her head. "I'm sorry, but I'm not sure who you are."

I laughed. "It seems my costume is doing its job a little too well." I briefly pulled my mask up so she could see my face.

Her eyes lit up in recognition. "Mr. Nelson! It's good to see you. How have you been?"

"Quite well," I replied, happy to have run into a familiar face. Flora Woodhouse had been the zeppelin pilot in charge of transporting Sky Manor contenders over to the floating island each year to compete. She was also the daughter of Mr. Woodhouse, Sky Manor's eccentric butler. I hadn't seen her or her father since the manor's demise.

"What have you been up to?"

"Oh, mostly trying to find work since you blew up my last job." She said it so drily I almost mistook the barb as serious—until she giggled. The sound was high-pitched and lasted a few seconds too long, reminding me very much of her father's odd mannerisms.

I wasn't sure whether to laugh along with her or apologize, so I settled on a neutral expression. "How is your father doing?"

She grinned and flicked her eyes behind me. "Why don't you ask him yourself?"

I spun around to find the quirky old man sauntering up to us. "Rupert, what on earth are you wearing? I nearly mistook you for that other fellow for a moment there."

I hid a smirk. My attire was much less ostentatious than the wild costume he was wearing. Some bizarre mishmash of cogs, tubes, and piano keys attached to a long-tailed coat and trousers that looked just as likely to explode as to burst into a sonata.

"Well, it *is* a masquerade party. It seems you didn't read the invitation," I teased, gesturing to his bare face.

He shrugged, eyes twinkling as if he knew something no one else did. "Ah, but isn't this the best disguise of all? Sometimes invisible masks conceal the most."

"Should I bother asking how you managed to get in here? I thought this was a party for the Elite only."

"And yet, here you are," Mr. Woodhouse pointed out.

Wes Acton passed through the crowd behind him, drawing my gaze. "I'm sorry, but I need to excuse myself. Maybe we can catch up more another time." I nodded to the Woodhouses in turn, then dashed out a door that opened onto a large veranda.

What in the—where did he go? I was sure that it had been Wes's flashy blond head ducking outside. I couldn't afford to lose him, not when he was my best chance at finding Camilla on this enormous estate.

"What's your problem?" came a low voice near the bushes, unmistakably Wes's.

I crept to the edge of the patio. I could just make out two men whispering by the bushes. Their hushed conversation drifted to my eager ears.

"The Carranza girl," the second man said, "is too much of a liability. I don't understand why you invited her."

"A good player can always use another pawn. Especially one desperate to become a queen. Tonight, we'll see if she has what it takes."

"And if she doesn't measure up?"

"Let's just say I have . . . insurance of a sort." Wes's voice was oily, seeping into the folds of my brain until I was inundated with fear.

The other man responded with a sinister laugh, then motioned for Wes to follow him back inside. Toward me.

I hurtled to the door and threw it open, not daring to look back until I'd pushed my way into the throng of people and slunk around one of the ballroom pillars. Wes said something to his associate, who quickly nodded before hastening off toward the main hallway. Once he was gone, Wes's attention turned to the ballroom, his eyes scanning the crowd like he was searching for—

I jumped back behind the column, heart careening in my chest. He'd seen me. The fact that I was in costume, and therefore unlikely to have been recognized, barely registered. Now Wes knew without a shadow of a doubt that someone was spying on him, and whatever "insurance" he had regarding Camilla may have just shifted from contingency to reality.

No more fooling around. I had to get Camilla out of here—now.

Chapter Eight

Camilla

The masquerade revolved around me like I was on some carousel ride spinning with no aim in mind. Colorful frocks shone in brilliant shades of aqua, emerald, creme, and rouge. The masks–oh the masks–were so ornate and delightful that I wanted to snatch them from the other guests' faces and take them home with me. Besides, pilfering would make it much easier to find the oval-faced boy who would die at my hand if the Elite had their way.

One older woman mingled among the crowd of party attendees. The lady who'd helped Horace spun into view with her giant feather over her head and her bare face in view. I inhaled sharply. Though years had passed since I'd last seen her, I'd never forget the face of Lady Arabella.

I found myself moving in her direction as if something deep inside of me had been longing to speak to her once again. Why did she have the poison all those years ago? Why had she paid for our school and continued to pay long after my sister's death? Though her poison had caused me the greatest pain I'd ever felt in my life, her scholarship had provided opportunities I never could have acquired on my own.

When I finally stood before her, looking her directly in the eye, I said in the most awkward manner any esteemed lady could have, "May I speak to you privately?"

Lady Arabella's gaze swept down my body and back to my face. "Do I know you?" She didn't bother putting a smile on her rouge-painted lips.

"Yes, I am Camilla Carranza."

Her skin blanched, and for a beat, she stilled. Would she pretend not to know my name, or would she admit recognition? I wasn't sure.

"Come to the study with me," Lady Arabella said in a curt tone that left me aching to reverse time and settle for finding Horace.

Lady Arabella gestured for me to follow her down a passageway with fine wood-paneled walls, polished and set with gas lamps to light the tiled black-and-white floors. The woman kept her head high with a cocky stride, as if she owned the mansion. An automaton rolled past us with a tray of flutes filled with bubbly beverages. I shifted to not tip the tray in any way. The older woman turned up a stairwell that appeared to be for the help. I followed close behind, now pulsing with nerves that screamed for me to run the other way.

"Where are we headed?" I asked.

In her aristocratic accent, she answered, "All that education, and you still don't know how to listen."

I swallowed my embarrassment at her accusation. It wasn't as if someone had told me not to take the poison in her purse when I was a little girl. Our heels clicked as they grazed the landing to the second floor. She turned left and continued her trek to the end of the passageway. There was a door with a golden handle and keyhole. She fitted a skeleton key into the lock and twisted.

Part of me recoiled, expecting a darkened room holding victims, but when she flipped the switch, the yellow light illuminated only a study lined with bookshelves. I slipped into the door she held open and admired the leather-bound spines all along the back wall behind a solid desk.

Lady Arabella slammed the door shut behind me and locked the door. "Sit."

I obeyed, taking the seat in front of the desk.

She marched around the desk, shut a cabinet with a row of films exposing a row of films, and slammed the key against the empty desk.

"I should have known that you would persist in haunting me. How much do you want?" She hunched beneath the desk, reaching until I heard a click.

"What do you mean?" I slipped off my mask so she could witness my shock at her response.

"No one is to know about my work in the poisons, child. I thought an education and connections with the Elite might satisfy you, but I see that they have not. When I saw you had participated in the Sky Manor game, I knew that you'd come back for me." She laid a pile of bank notes on the desktop. "I've worked too hard to get my husband and all of this for one incident to ruin me." Her beautiful features now twisted and deepened along wrinkle lines over her forehead.

"I think you mistake my intentions."

"Do I? Can you seriously tell me that you showed up to the Games because you didn't want fortune or fame?" Her nose flared with an angry accusation that I couldn't comprehend.

"Yes, you are correct"—my voice came out small and pitiful as if I'd reverted to the small child I once was—"but I don't see how my previous intentions have anything to do with you. I came to thank you for all you've done for my family despite me stealing from your purse."

Her lines smoothed over her face, and she leaned back in the giant chair.

"I've had so many questions about that day, but I think I understand now."

"Do you?" She grabbed a stack of notes and lopped the bound stack in front of me. "Then take this for your silence and be off with you." She scooped the other stacks and returned them to the secret compartment. "You turned out to be just as beautiful as I anticipated, but what else can be expected from a Vicario? Don't squander the assets God has given you."

My stomach churned like a nest of worms, writhing in guilt and questions. Vicario was Mamá's maiden name. Did this lady have another connection to me that I didn't know about? Either way, the veil was torn. This lady that I'd once esteemed wasn't who I wanted to be anymore. I had chosen Rupert instead of striving for jewels.

Lady Arabella stood and worked her way around the desk to sit in the chair beside me.

"Why are you here?"

In that moment, I could've lied. I should have lied. But if I wanted to be the opposite of the miserable woman beside me, I had to start choosing to be another person. "The Elite invited me to join their consortium."

"And what did they require of you?"

"To kill Horace."

"My husband and stepson don't like opposition to their ideas. I was wondering why Wes was so sure of the Games returning. I see why."

"Your husband and stepson?" I envisioned her helping Horace tie his mask in place.

"Mr. Acton and Wes, of course. This is my home."

The tender moment I had imagined a second before shattered into something malevolent. I cleared my throat and asked, "Will you tell them about this conversation?"

"No, just like you won't tell them about the poison and your sister's death."

"Of course."

"Let me tell you a little secret."

I wanted to shout at her to stop. She had already ruined my good opinion of her. I didn't need more secrets to destroy the woman I'd spent years trying to emulate.

"Since you're family, we already have a deep connection even though your mother chose to marry poor."

My mouth went dry as all my memories scattered and reorganized into understanding. When I'd told Mamá about Lady Arabella and the glass bottle, Mother had wiped her tears with a sudden shift in hot emotion. I'd thought she was angry at me, but she simply changed into her best dress to go for a private walk. When she'd returned, she'd explained that all her children had received a scholarship.

Now Lady Arabella placed me under her baleful stare. "I see that my secret is not so hidden from you already. Yes, I killed Wes's mother with that very poison in my purse. That's why I went to celebrate that day at the shop. It was a day of victory for me until *someone* stole my poison and gave your mother evidence against me."

My muscles tensed under her intense scrutiny as she gauged my response to her declaration. Remaining composed, I shifted my hand to the edge of the hard chair to keep it within easy reach of my pistol. "Why are you telling me this?"

"Because I want you to know that if you so much as whisper about this conversation or act against Wes, I will kill you myself in spite of the promises I made to Grandfather. And then, I will go to your house and put an end to your miserable family. Tonight, Wes offers you a great honor by having you join the most powerful family in the city, and you will be rewarded beyond your wildest dreams."

"I understand."

A smirk curled her lips, appearing far more innocent than it should. "I will help you. How do you plan to handle the matter? Poison?"

Trembling at her boldness, I lifted my chin higher and infused confidence into my posture. "No, I have a pistol."

"So messy." She wrinkled her nose in distaste for my choice of weapon. "Take my advice and do the deed out back in the hedge maze. It will be much easier for the automatons to clean."

I glanced out of the window and strained to make out more than the blurry orb light that stretched in the distance, giving no hint to how extensive this property actually was.

Lady Arabella continued to speak. "And as for the Games, you really should attend the next one. I will make sure to do what I can to keep you alive. My husband was upset at losing such an investment, but if I speak to him, he will withhold his anger from you." Her insinuation that I would even consider going back to a game where a person must die for riches heated my blood, yet I couldn't risk a display that might turn her against me. She was the epitome of wickedness.

"No, I won't attend another Game." I reached for her bank notes, which were placed beside the study key she had used to open the door. It shone like a beacon, calling me to collect it. I was no thief like my friend Jessie, but the itch grew in my fingertips with such close proximity.

"Well, that's a shame"—she turned to look at the door as if to give me room to take the notes without a witness—"but I suppose my husband can find another beauty to promote."

A war tugged within me between taking the key or leaving it behind. Another battle waged about whether or not to accept her lucrative offer. I covered the glittering key with my palm, but shook with fright at what I was doing.

"For all that is good over the Aether Sea, take the notes, or I'll have to assume you won't be silent." Her heels clicked over the floor as she neared the door.

I pinched the key in my grasp and swiped the notes with my other hand. Why was I so weak? I secured the loot in my dress skirt, making quick work of the button holding the pocket closed.

We left the room and walked together until we arrived at the stairs.

Lady Arabella swore. "I need to go back to the study. Do you remember the way out?"

With a nod, a tense smile stretched across my face. There was no going back to replace what I'd stolen. Now, I could only hope Lady Arabella concluded that she had misplaced her key. I'd never skipped down a stairway faster in my life.

Chapter Nine

Rupert

I spent the next half hour charging through the mansion like a rampaging bull. If anyone made the mistake of coming into my path, they took one look at my deliberate gait and moved out of the way before I plowed them over. Several guests grumbled about my lack of manners, but manners were the last thing on my mind right then. Where could Camilla have gone?

And then, there she was, a vision in a black mask and a brilliant red dress that highlighted her curves and contrasted perfectly with her warm brown skin. My heart stopped dead at the sight of her, Wes and his looming threat forgotten. She was just as breathtaking as the first time I'd laid eyes on her, sitting by the fountain at Saint Clockwell Preparatory Academy between classes. I'd known then and there that she was the one for me.

I spotted Wes in the far corner of the room, drinking out of a glass and happily chatting with a few other guests as if the conversation I'd overheard hadn't taken place. He glanced up and made eye contact with Camilla, who nodded and gave him a smile that sent a jolt through my chest.

I winced and dropped my gaze. Camilla wasn't in danger. Paranoia was getting the better of me. *Well done, Rupert. Well done. You only barely managed to keep yourself from looking like an idiot, crashing in here to rescue her when she doesn't even need rescuing.*

My heart rate slowed, and I looked down at my fancy suit and thick metal mask with a self-deprecating chuckle. Maybe I should have just agreed to come here with her in the first place. Then we could have been enjoying the evening together instead of me skulking about like some wannabe assassin.

Granted, the evening wasn't over yet. . . .

I started to walk over to her, but my legs locked in place at the sight of Camilla laughing with a young gentleman by the windows. She looked like she belonged here, more than she'd ever belonged with me.

But she'd *chosen* me. That had to count for something. Right?

I took a deep breath and sauntered over, head held high. The current song was just ending as I reached her, so I tapped her shoulder and whispered, "May I have the next dance?"

Camilla spun around with a gasp, hand pressed over her heart. When her gaze locked with mine, her lips twisted with disapproval. "I don't suppose you're here to convince me to return to the Sky Manor Games, too, are you?"

My eyes widened at her cold tone, but then I realized she didn't recognize me.

"Of course that's not why I'm here. I came to—" I clamped my mouth shut, a dangerous thought zipping through my head: *What am I doing? I can't afford to waste an opportunity like this. Now I can find out if she's truly as committed to me as she claims.*

I cleared my throat and deepened my voice a bit beyond its normal pitch. "I just wanted to dance with the most beautiful woman in the room, if she'll allow it." I held out my hand, praying she'd take it.

Camilla tentatively accepted my offer, but the suspicious gleam didn't leave her eyes as we got into position. I placed my free hand on the small of her back while she put hers on my shoulder. Her touch sent ripples of pleasure through me, but I reminded myself to stay focused on the goal. If she passed my test, I'd reveal myself afterward and then we'd have plenty of time to enjoy being together—the rest of our lives, in fact.

A slow, sweet tune filled the air, and the other dancers began to step, turn, and spin in the familiar style of a waltz. Perfect. I led my masked partner around the room with practiced precision, our movements as fluid as water. After a few minutes, Camilla seemed to relax a bit, her attention shifting from me to the rest of the room. But there was still a skittishness about her, as if she were afraid something bad was about to happen.

Was she feeling guilty for being here against my wishes?

"Do you come to events like these often?" I asked.

She tensed in my arms, hesitating to answer. "No, as a matter of fact, I don't." Her words were soft, careful, as if she were afraid of giving too much away.

"Then I should count myself blessed that you happened to be here tonight."

She drew in a sharp breath, eyes narrowing in annoyance. Had I said something wrong? I tried to think of how I might have offended her, but the only thing I could come up with was that maybe she didn't like that I'd used the word "blessed." A small portion of the Aetherfall population bore strange talents, like Wes's charm and Camilla's immunity to poison, and those individuals were called "the blessed."

I was one of the few Camilla had entrusted with her secret, and though many would have envied her for such a rare gift, Camilla resented it. Her immunity may have protected her from death as a child, but it hadn't spared her older sister.

I dipped her, the chandelier light descending upon her like snowflakes and drawing my attention to the smooth expanse of her neck. When she came back up, I leaned forward to kiss her, but then I remembered I was still wearing my mask and pulled away before she could notice the slip.

She glanced over my shoulder for a moment, then turned her gaze to me, lips pressed into a tight smile. "Don't be so quick to think our meeting is a good thing. For all you know, I could be planning to murder someone in this very room. Maybe even you." The words were more taunting than teasing despite her grin. But I caught a trace of something else in her tone, something I doubted she wanted me to hear: regret.

Camilla had opened up to me about her past dealing in poisons. It was what had led to her partnership with Arden Bentley, the fellow who'd died in the last Sky Manor Game. She'd concocted the poisons, while he'd passed them along to those looking for a quick way to get rid of their enemies. Was that what she was feeling bad about now? Or was it something more recent?

As soon as she finished a twirl, I swung her back into the circle of my arms, protectiveness surging through me. The song was ending, but I hesitated to release her. "Care to join me for another one?"

She pulled away. "I'm afraid not. There's actually someone I need to talk to."

"Ah, the boyfriend?" I jerked my chin toward Wes, who was not so subtly watching us from the side. I nearly smirked in triumph at the jealousy radiating off his face.

Camilla's lip curled back with disdain. "He's most definitely *not* my boyfriend. I have better taste than that."

I bit down a laugh, both from her incorrect word choice and from the relief bubbling up inside me. So, she wasn't going to let Wes sway her. In that case . . .

"Well," I began, my voice returning to its normal pitch, "then perhaps you and I should—"

"Excuse me, sir, but I really must get going. Thank you for the lovely dance." She dipped into a curtsey, then sashayed toward a group of guests.

"But, Camilla, I—" I broke off, skin prickling with an eerie sense of being watched. I swiveled around in all directions, trying to find the source of the feeling. My gaze swept to the corner where Wes had been just a moment ago, but he was already gone. Then who . . .?

A dark silhouette disappearing through the double doors grabbed my attention. Zenith?

I tramped after him into the hallway, my footfalls echoing against the checkerboard marble flooring. A few latecomers were making their way toward the ballroom, but the figure zigzagged around them with ease. Where was he going? Was he trying to find me? Or Camilla?

I retrieved my cloak from the automaton stationed in the hallway and threw it over my shoulders.

"Zenith, wait up!"

The hooded figure paused, glancing over a shoulder. I couldn't make out much of the face, but it was enough to know that it wasn't Zenith. I skidded to a stop and lifted an apologetic hand. "I'm sorry, I thought you were—"

A flash of white teeth stole my breath, the stranger's smile predatory and menacing. A low female voice rasped, "It's so nice to finally meet you, Rupert. My my, that's quite the get-up. I see my son's been rubbing off on you." The temperature in the room dropped as she pulled back her hood, the hairs on the back of my neck rising in terror.

Her feathery black hair was cut short, with a few strands framing a pale, angular face whose age was impossible to discern. A double-breasted swallowtail coat hung from her thin frame, its silver buttons like pinpricks of moonlight in the candlelit room. Her knee-high leather boots were nearly silent as she drifted nearer. Like a viper that could strike at any moment.

"Your-your son?" I stammered. I gripped the sides of my cloak, hoping she couldn't see my fear behind my mask.

She whipped a dagger out from one of her pockets and ran a long finger down its edge. "Tsk tsk, did dear Zenith not mention me?" Her eyes glimmered with malice. "How forgetful of him."

I gulped, pulse roaring in my ears. I didn't tell her Zenith *had* mentioned her, and it wasn't anything good. Zenith's mother was none other than the infamous Phoenix Lazarus, a hitwoman known for her exceptional skills and ruthless methods. She was also presumed to be dead.

Zenith, myself, and a few others were the only ones who knew otherwise, and not too long ago, Zenith had even tasked me with hiding a bomb for him—a bomb Phoenix had wanted for herself.

"It's . . . very nice to meet you, too," I stuttered, backing up slowly even though my gut told me it was a wasted effort.

The woman's eyes tracked my movements, but she didn't seem worried about my retreat. Quite the opposite, actually, judging by the amusement twitching at her lips. As if I were a rabbit trying to escape a tiger.

"My son isn't the type to make friends, so you must have impressed him quite a lot." Her gaze traveled up and down my form. "Though I don't see what's so impressive about a boy who made a living sneaking test answers and alcohol to his classmates."

All the blood left my face. How did she know about that? This woman was growing more dangerous by the second. I thought I'd buried my past so deep no one could uncover it.

Phoenix perched the tip of her dagger against her lip, expression contemplative. "On the other hand, you did have the wherewithal to blow up Sky Manor, so perhaps you're not as useless as you look."

"Um . . . thank you?" I glanced behind me at the doors leading to the ballroom. Could I make a run for it?

When I turned back, the woman's mouth had spread into a full smirk. "For Zenith's sake, I'll let you go this time, but know this: my generosity has limits. Stay out of my way, or you won't live long enough to regret it." She threw her hood back over her face and stalked off before my brain could register her threat.

This evening had just gone from bad to worse. Wes Acton was someone to be wary of; Phoenix Lazarus was on a completely different level. Seeing her here could only mean she had business at the Acton estate.

I just hoped it had nothing to do with Camilla; otherwise, I doubted I'd be able to protect her.

Chapter Ten

Camilla

Time was running out. Why had I wasted my night waiting for Horace to invite me to dance? The last fellow had had my skin crawling from the look of his iron mask and the ridiculous rasp he'd forced into his voice, yet he'd smelled of vanilla and spices like Rupert. Could it be him?

I scanned the crowd for another glimpse of the strange fellow. No, Rupert would have stayed to protect me and to make sure

I wasn't doing something untoward. Guilt coiled within my stomach.

An automaton rolled around me with a tray of flutes again, so I snatched one and downed the beverage as quickly as possible. The bubbly drink tumbled down my throat, not even pleasant to the taste.

A few male onlookers stared from the wall nearest me with admiration shining in their eyes. Dunstan stood among them with his mask pulled to his forehead, and he had the audacity to wink at me. I marched onward, taking in a lungful of air to settle the jitters in my bones. I found a corner and settled onto a cushioned chair by myself. Should I leave to keep myself from further trouble? But Horace still needed to know about the threat to his life.

God, You've got to hear me. I am trying to change, but I still have the stolen key and banknotes burdening one pocket and my easy-to-reach pistol in the other. The fact that I'd even tailored my gowns to have secret compartments seemed like evidence enough that I should be struck dead.

Twirling couples continued to move through the dance floor when Horace finally appeared at the end of the room greeting a group of young masked guests. I got to my shaky feet, now throbbing from the points of my shoes. Movement to my left caught my attention. The older women were moving closer to the dancers to join in the merriment for the next song. Lady Arabella was among the couples, holding tight to an austere older man's arm with a larger version of Wes's nose and a thick, tidy mustache popular among the wealthiest of men.

I quickened my pace to Horace and away from Lady Arabella's view. The closer I got, the more I recognized Horace's friends. One fellow had an angular face that couldn't be hidden behind his ill-fitting mask. One girl had a mass of unruly curls she was trying to hide beneath a layer of feathers meant to look like a peacock's. They'd been classmates with wealthy connections but had an unpopular standing in school, like Horace. I entered their circle and pretended to laugh alongside them as if someone had told a joke.

Dozens of stares landed on me, and their smiles flipped. I pressed my palms over my stomach from a sudden wave of queasiness. Though I hadn't expected a sudden welcome, I'd hoped to be less of a spectacle.

"I need to speak to Horace. It's of the utmost—"

He came to my side, but with the mask on, I was unable to decipher his mood. A curly-haired girl narrowed her gaze at me and dragged a finger across her throat as if she'd slash my throat if I misbehaved. After Lady Arabella's real threat, this one came across as comical, so much so that I chuckled. In response to my laughter, the girl marched in my direction but was blocked by the slender fellow.

"Perhaps, we should have this conversation out in the garden," I suggested to Horace.

Horace smoothed a hand over his face as if he were annoyed. "No. Camilla, I understand that Ben is in prison and that you've gone through a big ordeal, but I am not the type of person who needs a beautiful lady on my arm to make me feel better about myself."

"Good," I said. "That's not why I need to speak to you."

He removed his mask, showing his lightly freckled cheeks and childish edges that hadn't finished settling into his adult features. "Then, what could *you* possibly want from the ugly duckling from fifth hour Literature?"

Heat inched up my neck at him repeating the words I'd so boldly said to a friend without consideration of who might have heard them. "I'm sorry for how I behaved in the past. It was wrong what I said, and I don't believe those words to be true."

"Did you find out who my dad is?" he asked. "Are you hunting for the next rich man to fall for you? Everyone knows why you dated Ben Nelson."

"I am trying to save your life," I said between gritted teeth.

His screwed-up lips slackened, and he visibly swallowed. "Maybe we should go to the garden, after all."

"Thank you." I looped my arm around his elbow and couldn't resist looking back at his feral friend. The curly-haired girl continued to watch us as Horace walked me to the back doors, and I bit my bottom lip to keep from taunting her. That was what the old Camilla Carranza would have done to make sure the girl knew her place in the pecking order. Yet now my behavior reminded me too much of Lady Arabella. Instead, I searched the crowd to see if Wes or Lady Arabella had witnessed our departure.

Lady Arabella remained occupied as her husband led her around the dance floor. Wes was out of view.

Horace guided me out of a doorway to a terrace that overlooked a sculpted hedge maze.

When we exited the building, I shivered from the cool night air. This was exactly where Lady Arabella wanted me to do away with Horace. Was I falling into her game?

Chapter Eleven

Camilla

Gaslamps burned atop the expansive hedge maze behind the grand estate. On one end of the garden, a plaque had bright gold letters with the words: START HERE. On the far end, some fifty yards away, a plaque read: THE END. A brick wall seemed to encircle the estate—at least the parts that I could see in the darkness. Though some stars peeked at us from above, a haze of light emanated from Aetherfall and stole the deep blue hue of night from the sky.

Horace rounded on me and said in the harshest tone I'd ever heard breach his lips, "Please explain yourself."

My mouth went dry, and I crossed my arms to warm myself. "It's like I said."

"I am the proconsul's son. When is my life ever not in danger?" He removed his red jacket, revealing a crème-colored undershirt with the sheen of expensive cotton. "Take my coat."

"Thank you." I wrapped his wool-and-silk-stitched jacket over my body, warmed by his kind gesture. "Horace, I don't know how to say this, but the Elite plans to do away with you."

"It's all over the newspapers that my father is at odds with the council members. I'm going to need a little more information than that."

I averted my gaze from Horace, still wracked with guilt over how he'd heard me call him an ugly duckling, but then I caught a lamp reflecting off something metallic in the shadows. My creepy dance partner shifted in the shadows and returned to the terrace. Even with Horace's silky coat, a legion of goosebumps rose along my arms.

Horace followed my line of sight. "An admirer of yours?"

"No. I danced with him earlier, and I'm not sure what to make of him. Perhaps we should enjoy the hedge maze and keep moving?" I nudged Horace's side. "Do you need your jacket back?"

He eyed the iron-masked man still watching us from afar with a furrowed brow. "No, I don't. Let's go into the maze. I'm assuming this means you have something more to say."

"I do." I passed the plaque and paused for a moment. Words scrambled in place to form a small poem on the entrance sign:

START HERE
To find the hidden gardens
Be warned of the sound at each new place
A path in silence each bell toll might erase
Those who wander win at the end of the maze

"Creepy, wouldn't you say?" Horace broke through my thoughts and dragged me over the threshold of the maze. "Don't worry, I've completed this conundrum before."

"Perhaps we could find somewhere inside to speak," I said.

"If secrecy is what you want, then the maze is the only way we're getting away from prying ears and automatons." Horace took a quick left and led the way around a corner.

"I don't believe my one pistol will put an end to whatever foul tricks they put in this place." I kept pace with Horace's long gait, though the shadows reminded me of the secret passages in Sky Manor and the cloying sensation of being trapped. "We should go back now."

"Camilla, you can't take the poem seriously. It's just a garden. And you have a pistol on hand?" Horace had a playful lilt in his voice that was off-putting.

"Horace, stop." I grabbed his forearm, which was much stronger than I'd anticipated, and dug my heels into the grass. "Let's go back."

He spun around and raked a hand through his hair. "Fine, this should be out of audio range for automatons and Scary Mask. Seriously, what do you know about the Elite and them wanting me dead? Tell me something I don't know."

"Well—" I dug my fingers more into the jacket—"Wes asked me to join, but required that I dispatch you."

Horace's eyes popped wide, allowing the firelight to pick up a rich brown color.

A bell sounded. The garden shook beneath our feet, and the hedge walls shifted, cutting off our previous trail and opening two new paths. Once the rumble had stopped, all that was left were the sounds of Horace's and my deep breaths and the distant orchestra music echoing from somewhere in the distance.

Fear gripped my stomach with an iron fist. Someone had shifted the hedge walls, or perhaps something supernatural existed here like the plaque insinuated. Either way, we had to find a way to escape.

Horace shifted his jaw; whatever playfulness had been there before now had no bearing on his current countenance. "So, they sent you to kill me." There was no question in his statement, only the chilling acceptance of the truth.

"I'm not planning on actually harming you; I just thought you needed to know."

Branches cracked somewhere to our right, and both of us whipped our heads around.

"Let's keep moving." Horace put a guiding hand on my shoulder as we traversed deeper into the new maze layout with only the haze of the night sky and torches for guidance. "What are the consequences if you don't comply with Wes's request?"

My feet continued to move as we hurried around corners, only to find more leafy walls. "They'll accuse me of poisoning Arden in the Sky Manor Game."

We turned another bend, and a fountain appeared past the end of the walkway. Horace's firm hand pressed on my shoulder, irking me in its pushiness but keeping us tethered just in case the maze shifted again. Upon breaching the opening, we raced to the solid-looking fountain.

Horace overtook me and craned his head down to look into the water as if he was searching for something in it. When I reached his side again, I expected water within the stone confines, but only found blue tiles in circular designs.

"You know, Camilla, I thought we were Literature friends." His admonition felt like an arrow to the heart. "But when I heard you telling everyone that I was the ugly duckling and how you used me to get ahead in school, I was hurt."

"I'm sorry." My cheeks burned with sorrow for what I'd done to someone who still chose kindness after my cruelty. "I was a fool. Please forgive me."

"Are you part of the reason the maze shifted? Is this your way of getting a good name with the Elite, making me feel like you're doing me a favor and then shooting me in the middle of the maze?"

I took a step backward at his accusation. "Horace, please. I needed to tell you that they want you dead by tomorrow. I'm not sure why, but if I had to guess, it's something to do with the game maker and city councils wanting to bring back the Game. They have evidence against me, and I made a mess of things when I stole this key to the study." I produced the glittering key from my pocket, now feeling the weight of having done a real crime tonight. "I guess, after I saw the film cans, I thought maybe the evidence was there, and if there was no proof, then I could be free."

A flash of recognition sparked in his eye, and he pinched the bridge of his nose. "My father was right about keeping my mouth shut. We've got to get out of here."

"How?"

"What if I climb up the water spout and see how close we are to a wall? You might have to do a little climbing."

The beautiful fabric of my dress with the silk and layers beneath the skirt could get torn, but before I'd agreed to his plan, he'd already climbed the stone center of the fountain. He pointed to our left. "Over there."

On his way down, he leaped before me and gave me a lopsided grin. "You're forgiven. But hey, you aren't in the clear either. I have some files on Wes's family that could get them in big trouble should they leak to the public. It might be just what you need to stay out of prison."

I nodded, now hopeful that this nightmare might have a simple end.

The telltale sound of footfalls approached from somewhere behind us.

"Come on, before the maze shifts again." Horace took my hand in his, and we bolted.

We had to make it before whomever was following caught us or the maze shifted. With that thought, a bell tolled and a creaking noise cut through the air. The bush walls squeezed in on us. Horace sprinted.

I lifted my skirt and stomped my foot into the grass to pick up the pace when I was yanked back by my own shoe stuck in the grass.

Chapter Twelve

Rupert

It seemed I was going to spend the entire evening chasing my girlfriend down. After Zenith's mom left me, I dashed back to the ballroom, determined to get Camilla out of there even if I had to drag her kicking and screaming. But the only person I found dressed in red was a matronly woman scarfing down hors d'oeuvres like she hadn't eaten in weeks.

I ran a hand through my thick hair. Was I too late? Had Phoenix gotten to her? No, that was impossible. Phoenix had walked *away* from the ballroom, not toward it. She couldn't have gotten to Camilla already . . . could she?

Calm down. For all you know, Phoenix isn't even here for Camilla. I tried to slow my breathing, telling myself all would be well, but my efforts were in vain. As long as Camilla was here, my heart couldn't rest.

"Excuse me," I called to a passing servant with a wispy gray beard, "I danced with a young woman in a red dress a short while ago. Did you happen to see her?"

The older man shook his head and gestured to the empty tray in his hand. "I just got here, and I already need to get more drinks. You might ask that servant over there. She's due for a reprieve in a few minutes." He pointed to a willowy young woman on the other side of the room.

"Much obliged." I strode over to the second servant, who stood at one of the small tables. A wet spot soaked the front of her lacy white apron, and her hands shook as she rearranged shrimp on a silver platter.

I cleared my throat. "Excuse me."

She cringed as she spun around. "Y-yes? Can I help you, sir?" She kept her body hunched forward as if she wanted to make herself as small as possible.

"I hate to bother you, but did you see a young woman pass through here a few minutes ago? She was wearing a red dress and a black mask."

The servant nodded a few times. "Yes, sir. She went that way toward the hedge maze."

I thanked her and hurried off, my boots clomping against the polished wooden floorboards. Why would Camilla have gone out there?

A crisp wind lifted my cloak as I stepped into the night air and scanned the grounds. The hedge maze sprawled out across the back of the estate like a giant spider web, with seemingly arbitrary twists and turns that made my head spin. I'd never been good at finding my way around and had gotten lost in the city more times than I cared to admit. The odds I'd somehow find Camilla *and* my way back out were slim to none.

But I had to try.

A couple whispered at the entrance beside a large plaque I assumed gave the directions for how to navigate the maze. The man shrugged off his coat and handed it to his da—

My stomach hardened. That wasn't his date; that was Camilla!

I clenched my teeth so hard pain shot through my jaw. What did he think he was doing with *my* girlfriend? I stomped forward, ready to knock the fellow off his feet, but then Camilla's gaze shot to mine. Instead of looking relieved at my presence, she drew back nervously and bumped her shoulder against the stranger's.

The young man's head swiveled in my direction, giving me a better view of his pudgy face. Wasn't he one of our old classmates?

He mumbled something to Camilla, who was moving into the maze.

"No, wait," I called, but they didn't react, my words lost in the wind. I cursed under my breath as they disappeared into the dark mass of shrubbery. I jogged up to the entrance, stopping short at the ominous welcome sign.

> START HERE
> Move quickly, but quietly
> In these walls of illusion,
> Hold tight to your perception
> to avoid all confusion
> One step forward, two steps back
> Truth prevails over deception

I rolled my shoulders, trying not to let my anxiety get the better of me. But *why* did it have to be a riddle? Why couldn't it just tell me which way to go? I'd had more than my fair share of riddles at Sky Manor, and I wasn't keen on dealing with any more.

Come on, Rupert. It's just a bunch of bushes, nothing more.

But before I could muster the courage to step inside, a strange rustling emanated from within, and one of the hedge walls shifted to the right, removing the path that had been there seconds before.

Camilla. She was trapped! I raced onto the newly formed path, heart in my throat.

God, if You're listening, please . . . help me find her.

The hedge walls didn't move again as I hurried along the edge of the maze, so maybe my prayer was working. I didn't enjoy tight spaces, not after I'd been locked in a closet overnight once at school. I had Wes and my cousin Ben to thank for that lovely incident.

I took a left, moving deeper into the green labyrinth. Clouds gathered above, concealing the moon from view so the only light came from the torches scattered about the hedges. I wiped my sweaty hands on my trousers. I needed to get to the center, right? That was the way mazes typically worked. No shortcuts.

Crackling just ahead was the only warning I got before the hedge wall next to me swerved, pushing me along with it. I fell to the ground, leaves and branches pressing against my hair and clothes until they reached their designated position. I coughed a few times and stood, brushing dirt off my stained clothes.

"Should have just worn my old suit," I muttered.

Voices on the other side of the hedge interrupted my complaining, and I shuffled forward to hear better.

". . . they want you dead by tomorrow," Camilla was saying.

What? Was that why Wes had invited her to this charade? To persuade her to murder someone?

I refocused on her words, not wanting to miss something vital.

". . . I stole this key to the study. I guess, after I saw the film cans, I thought maybe the evidence was there, and if there was no proof, then I could be free."

My heart stopped. What? Evidence against Camilla? What sort of evidence could she be talking about?

Film cans . . . Wes's family was one of many Elite families backing the Sky Manor Games. Could he have gotten hold of footage from our time there? But Camilla hadn't killed Arden. The films clearly showed my cousin Ben pushing him to his death.

Except, if Wes had access to Sky Manor's films, he could choose *which* footage to give the police and which to withhold. And Arden had mistakenly drunk one of Camilla's poisoned vials before Ben's final shove.

The ground rumbled beneath my feet, and I leaped forward just before the path collapsed in on itself, leaving a gaping hole where I'd been standing. I pressed a hand over my heart, trying to calm myself. Who designed this thing? This maze was way too dangerous to be a rich man's diversion.

A high-pitched scream snapped me back to my senses, and I bolted down a new path I hoped would lead to the source. The path opened up to a circular area with a fountain at its center, and there, lying on the ground with a vine around her ankle, was a familiar figure in red.

I pulled a knife from my pocket, glad I'd had the forethought to arm myself, and ran over.

At the sound of my approach, Camilla rolled over, eyes widening when she saw me. "Stay back," she warned, hand reaching for something under her dress. When she drew it out again, she was holding a pistol. She pointed it at my chest. "If you come any closer, I'll shoot."

"You don't need to—"

"Don't speak!" Her voice shook, but her aim remained steady. She'd always been a good shot. And rather unpredictable. If I tried to remove my mask, would she shoot me before she realized who I was?

I wasn't about to risk it, so I closed my mouth and lifted my hands to show I meant no harm.

Camilla's chest heaved, drawing my gaze to the scratches tracing down her collarbone. The maze hadn't been kind to her.

When she next spoke, her voice was steely, any former weakness swallowed up by determination. "Now, you're going to hand over that knife very slowly, and then you're going to go tell whoever sent you that no one is killing Camilla Carranza tonight."

I did as she urged, not breathing a word as our fingers brushed in the transfer. Even in this vulnerable state, she was a force to be reckoned with, and despite my fear, I couldn't help but feel a surge of admiration. She was bold in all the ways I wasn't.

And I needed her desperately.

Whatever she was up to, with Wes, with that other guy—where had he gone?—all I knew in that moment was that I loved her too much to stop her. She'd always been headstrong; trying to keep her from doing what she wanted was usually a losing battle anyway.

But perhaps I could help her. I reached for the strings at the back of my mask. "Camilla, I need to—"

Her narrowed eyes returned to mine, freezing me in place. "Did you forget what I said so quickly? Go on before I decide your dead body will get the message across better." She gestured with her gun toward the path I'd come from.

I ducked my head but didn't protest, walking off into the maze until I'd turned the corner and was no longer in her line of sight.

I stopped, not sure where to go from here. Should I follow Camilla from a distance? She'd likely shoot me if she noticed my presence, maybe before I'd gotten a chance to identify myself.

Something sparkled in the torchlight. Had Camilla lost an earring? I bent down to retrieve it, but my hand closed around something long and thin that brought back a host of unpleasant memories—a solid gold key.

This must be the key I'd overheard her whispering about with that old classmate. What had she said? Something about how it unlocked the study where the incriminating film cans were stored.

I started to turn around to give it back to her, then paused, remembering the distrust in her gaze. Would it have been any different if I hadn't been wearing this mask? She'd gone behind my back to attend this uppity charade, after all.

That old, familiar anger poked at me. How could she still not trust me after everything we'd been through?

But then Zenith's insightful words sprang up in my mind: *"I think Camilla loves you, but until she knows the truth about the fortune you've come into, she's going to keep looking for ways to secure your future. Whatever that may look like."*

The truth sank in my stomach, heavy as a stone. She didn't believe I could take care of her. Why would she when I'd not done anything to allay her fears? In her eyes, I was still a poor shopkeeper, a nobody just barely making ends meet, not someone she could rely on.

That was why she'd come tonight—because *my* lack of trust had forced her to grasp at straws.

I swayed on my feet, reaching out to the nearest hedge wall to support myself. Shame spread through my limbs, numbing me from the inside out. No wonder Wes's invitation had been so tempting. It was the first real hope she'd had, since I'd refused to tell her the truth. I'd let her struggle needlessly, worry needlessly, and for what? Because I'd been afraid she might not love the real me and just want me for my money?

Wes was right. I was an absolute dog.

I looked up, only to glimpse the Acton mansion just ahead. Somehow I'd wound up back where I'd started.

No. Not where I'd started. I refused to be the coward I'd been before. But even now, fear battled against hope, paralyzing me as it had so many times throughout my life. I squeezed my hands into fists, feeling the cool metal of the key in my grip.

It was more than I could handle on my own. Already I could feel myself sinking, slipping under its looming shadow—

The clouds broke overhead, illuminating the path in a sudden beam of moonlight. A silent reminder that I wasn't alone, after all.

I tilted my head toward the heavens, hope rising victoriously in my chest. "God, I've been afraid all my life," I prayed solemnly. "Help me cast out that fear right now so I can finally be the man Camilla deserves."

Resolve drifted over me, soaking my skin in a gentle warmth that felt like a touch from above. I smiled and shifted my attention to the mansion. No longer was it a source of dread; now it was simply an obstacle to overcome. And overcome it, I would.

Where was that study?

Chapter Thirteen

Camilla

As if in slow motion, bushes on both sides of me closed in. Horace stopped and raced back to retrieve me. My foot ached from being held back by the gem-studded leather. I slipped out of my heels and went barefoot through the moist grass. The ground beneath me shifted, making every step treacherous.

"Come on, Camilla." Horace snatched my wrist as I threaded myself through colliding bush walls. We dodged a faster moving hedge and stormed into a dark mass of steady nothing. In this light, we couldn't make out the form.

The closer we got, the more distinct the vines appeared stretching high on the stone bricks. Horace dove for the wall. I leaped from a step behind him and slammed into the pokey branches and leaves.

Catching our breath, we clung to the boughs while the whole world shifted behind us. Movement ceased. I caught sight of my trembling, empty hand. Lady Arabella's key was gone, and so were my chances of retrieving the films from Sky Manor. The slow tumble of defeat slid down my throat and clutched my stomach.

Why had I ever thought I could control the situation with Wes? And who was the masked fellow?

A quiet fell over the garden as if the space were simply an innocent maze meant for partygoers to enjoy.

"That was close," Horace said under his breath.

"So, what now?"

"We climb." Horace ascended easily and rolled over the top wall. "Come on, more people are coming." He pointed behind me to where the shouts of people pierced the night.

"Couldn't we slip out of the front entrance? No one is watching." My limbs trembled even more now than when the maze had shifted. "I don't think this was such a good idea."

"We haven't time for a different plan, and honestly, I think they trust the maze will prevent us from escaping. There are guards and automatons everywhere."

I stepped onto a higher branch, feeling my weight bend the tiny arm. A small crack met my ears. One look down weaseled a small gasp out of my throat and ignited a spike of fear. My vision spun with the small distance from the grassy ground. I reached farther up, clinging to a weeping branch that could break at any moment. "I don't think this is going to work."

"A group of partygoers is getting closer. This isn't that tall of a wall."

"I'm moving as fast as I can, but I'm not a daredevil when it comes to heights."

"You're not even five feet from the ground." His voice had a tinge of amusement dancing along the edges of his words.

"Horsy, this wasn't my idea. Even if I get to the top, there is no way I can climb down the other side, which I'm sure is a sheer brick wall."

"You've resorted to name-calling," he teased.

"I can't."

Rustling and twigs snapping overhead caught my attention. Horace's face appeared above me with all ease and the hint of a crooked smile. The way the lamplight touched his round cheeks and straight nose made him appear almost handsome—that also might have been the dizziness speaking.

"Grab my hands, and I'll pull you up," he said.

Before I could second-guess his command, I took hold of his strong grip. He yanked me over the side, and I landed atop the wall. The dark path below me appeared stories high, and the maze was a small spectacle with a clear marked trail.

Cogs churned, and the walls within the hedge maze shifted. Female screams and male whoops rangthrough the night air.

"We should go," Horace said from directly in front of me.

I snapped my gaze at him.

We were head-to-head, lying flat over the thick wall. On one side of the barrier, there was a sheer drop with nowhere to place a foot.

"Let me go first." Horace let a slow smile cock up one side of his face, deepening a dimple I'd never noticed before.

"I won't jump."

"I'll catch you."

"No, you won't. You hate me and are going to drop me and leave me for dead."

"You're quite dramatic, you know?" He chuckled and rolled off the ledge.

Slamming my eyes closed, I turned away, unable to witness his self-imposed death.

"Camilla," he whisper-shouted up to me, "hang off the side, and I'll tell you when to let go." He stood at the bottom with his arms stretched up to me.

Footfalls marched from around the estate's corner. A man dressed in guard livery approached. With so many long shadows, I couldn't make out if it was one of Wes's men or just another stranger with a smart mustache.

Horace dropped his arms and turned to face the guard. "Hello, good sir."

"May I ask—oh, is it you, Horace?" the man asked.

"Yes, my date seems to have had such a fright from the moving maze that she got herself into a conundrum."

The man looked up at me, shaking his head.

Horace dropped his voice so much that I had to strain to hear what he said to the man. "Please, could you keep this encounter a secret between us? The lady will lose her good reputation, and I prefer no one knows where I've gone. You know how it is?"

"Yes, yes, but you should get down now before one of Mister Acton's guards does their round. There's another guard around the corner, but I'll give you some time."

"Thank you, I owe you."

The older man laughed. "You better hope she lands like a cat." He marched away, still shaking his head. "Kids these days."

My fingers clawed into the stone bricks so hard that circulation ceased, but I wouldn't ease my hold.

"Come on, Camilla, you heard the man. If you don't let go, you'll be stuck there for life."

"I can't believe you convinced me to do this." To my left, cogs churned with the shifting maze. I could make out figures coming into view, and one face with his hardened jaw and blond styled hair sharpened as the light angles touched it in different degrees. Wes Acton. My masked attacker was gone.

On impulse, I shifted my legs off the sheer stone brick side. My feet scrambled for purchase, but didn't find it.

"Let go," Horace called to me.

Clinging for dear life, I watched the figures in the maze turn a corner only ten feet from me. Lamplight glimmered over Wes.

When the man turned, I gasped. Wes's gaze scanned his new path and finally landed on me.

I let go of the stone brick and fell.

Cool night air rushed beneath my dress but did nothing to slow my descent. Hands grasped for my waist, but one of my flailing elbows struck something hard.

Horace grunted, but I hadn't time to think until, finally, a jolt of hard ground rattled my bones. I opened my eyes to find I had landed in a sitting position atop Horace. I dug through the layers of underdress to discover a bloody-nosed Horace wincing.

"I'm so sorry. Are you all right? Did you hit your head?" I got to my knees beside the fellow, with guilt wound so tightly in my chest that I thought my heart might hammer from its cage. It seemed I might kill my classmate, after all—but by accident, thanks to my fear of heights.

He winced and sat up. By the way he grabbed at the back of his head, I was certain he had a lump forming.

"Do you have butter and salt?" The words flew out of my mouth before I had a chance to consider how they sounded.

"What? Are you planning on basting me for dinner?"

"No, you fool, I'm trying to figure out how to stop the swelling on your head. You certainly must have a lump."

"There's a lump, all right."

I got to my feet and reached out an arm, nervous we might have signaled our escape from the estate to Wes.

Horace took my hand and leaned a little too hard into getting up, nearly toppling me over again. His unsteady feet told me that we wouldn't make it very far. He smoothed a hand over his face and pinched the bridge of his bloodied nose.

"Do you know of a café in this area?" I asked.

"Are you asking me out on a date?" Horace cut a glance at me through his pained expression.

"Don't get so excited; you're paying."

"I knew you were a gold digger." He chuckled as if that were some lighthearted joke, but the moment he met my eye, he sobered. "I prefer to return to my home. It's not too far from here."

Horace led us around a corner, and we walked in silence. The buildings all clustered on top of each other, but people were sparse. We made it to a wider intersection and turned up on a mountain side that overlooked the city. The wealthiest constituents lived in this sector of Aetherfall.

Horace watched me with amusement in his gaze. "This is what dreams aspire to achieve."

"What is?"

"Walking home with the most gorgeous girl from preparatory." His lips spread into a warm smile that touched his eyes in such a way that made every one of his features lovely. Perhaps it was the compliment or that I felt bad for the fellow, but either way, I couldn't let him know his comment touched me.

"So, you aspire to have your preparatory crush tell you news about an assassination attempt against you, then give you a bloody nose and try to take you out while falling from a brick wall?" I cocked an eyebrow high.

A silly grin overtook his face. "I'd like to point out that you are attempting to save my life, and you are alone with me and smiling. I call those both wins."

We continued our march up the mountain road, and several beats passed where we didn't speak.

"My father has been fighting the council about the Sky Manor Games for years. He plans to elevate me to a position on the council. With me, the current council votes will tip in my father's favor, rendering the Sky Manor Games illegal."

"Then I am for you joining the council, but I'm still under the Elite's thumb. They have evidence against me."

"What is it?"

"Poison."

Horace smoothed a hand over his face. "What's the evidence?"

"Arden's body."

"What if I told you that none of the video footage shows you poisoning him and there's no way they could have retrieved his body?"

My eyes lit up with a hope I hadn't felt all night long. "Could this be true? How would you know?"

"I saw the footage and reports. I will notify my lawyer to help you with any new accusations made."

In my enthusiasm, I placed my hand over his and squeezed.

He looked down at my gesture, calculation stirring in the shift of his jaw. "If it's not too presumptuous, could I ask you out on a date? A real one, that is?"

I slid my hands away from his. "About that. I am currently seeing someone. I understand if you don't want to help me anymore. It's just that my heart is taken."

He bent his head low. "It was a long shot, but I had to try. Of course, I'll still help you. It's the right thing to do."

"Horace, just know that I would have said yes otherwise." I bit my lip, surprised that I had admitted that to him and that my statement was true.

Though Horace smiled, it wasn't the same jubilant one he'd worn moments ago. "Here is my estate. It's probably the safest place for me to be anyway with the Elite so set on my death. While I'm hiding out, I'll write a reference letter to my lawyer on your behalf."

"Thank you."

One look at the guards lining the manor's gated entrance, and all my worries drained away. We were safe, and I had been imagining the worst for no reason whatsoever.

"Would you like a change of clothes?" Horace asked.

Under the atrium lamplight, I appraised the state of my red gown with the intricate flower pattern and flattering stitching. A tear ran just above one hem on my right side, and some dirt had smudged across my knees.

"I don't ask because of how it looks. It's just that everyone saw you in the gown, and though I plan on escorting you home in a coach, it would make you less noticeable if you wore something different. I will send a decoy in your dress out for a stroll."

Wes had threatened me, and after seeing me atop a wall, he surely would send a tail after us. I should have listened to Rupert and not attended the masquerade. What had I been thinking?

A stout man wearing thick goggles and a bow tie approached. A green light flashed on the corner of the man's eyepiece, and he removed the monstrous contraption on his face to reveal a set of heavy-lidded brown eyes.

Horace leaned close to my ear. "Night goggles with identity protection. It's the latest technology." He winked at me.

I snapped my gaped mouth closed and lifted my chin.

Horace continued, "You appear to be about the same size as my sister, so I'm sure we could find something suitable for you." He gestured for the butler and whispered something in the older man's ear.

"Will do, sir." The butler fled the room, leaving Horace and me alone in a giant round room with stairs to the left and right. A giant chandelier hung from a high ceiling and provided us with ample light to see just how rumpled we'd gotten.

"A maid can assist you in my sister's quarters while I retrieve the evidence for your innocence from the upstairs study. Do you want to see it?"

I bobbed my head, grateful that he, of all people, would choose to help me and for no other reason than it being the right thing to do.

A young woman exited a doorway wearing a simple gown and bonnet. She must have been asleep before this, but she smiled and led me up the stairs. Horace followed closely behind, not leaving me alone in this enormous mansion.

Upon passing stained wooden doors with decadent molding, Horace stopped. "Come here after you've changed." He looked past me to the maid. "Thank you, Gertrude."

"Of course, Sir Horace," the maid said. She led the way through a darkened room and into a closet bigger than my current bedroom, which I shared with my younger sister. "Choose any gown from this shelf. Wendy doesn't like to repeat what she wears at big events, so she won't notice or care if it's gone."

Any lingering doubts about Wes got squashed when the maid said, "Would you like to try them on?"

Lifting my dropped jaw from witnessing such a lavish lifestyle, I let myself gush over the fabrics with gold stitched patterns, flowers, and bodices woven with lace. Though fear gnawed at my gut, I tried on three different dresses, telling myself that I had to make sure there would be no wardrobe malfunctions from the different body styles. I ended up with a white dress with gold accents and a bodice woven with gold thread and lace. It came with a matching mask that satisfied the little girl inside of me, yet I didn't want to risk losing the gem-studded black one. My pockets weren't big enough for an extra mask, so to my frustration, I passed on putting the white one on my face.

Gertrude left me at the doors to the study and fled, yawning as if she had a date with her bed. I entered the room and headed toward the desk. The cushioned chair was turned away—that must be where Horace was seated. A musty scent stole some of the bewitching elements of the room, but I continued to move forward. I hadn't any idea that Horace was a smoker. He breathed hard with a rattling sound that was more like someone with asthma than a smoker's cough.

"Horace, I'm sorry I took so long." I bridged the gap between my classmate and I, now suddenly covered with goosebumps. "Horace? Horace, answer me." I turned the chair, but only brown leather cushions with brown leather buttons met my eye.

That was when I noticed Horace's body lying on the floor at the opposite end of the desk. A bloody wound covered the left side of his chest.

CHAPTER FOURTEEN

Rupert

THE STUDY HAD TO be on the upper floor, but that area was strictly off-limits to guests. *That doesn't matter now*, I reminded myself. I'd successfully sneaked into this party, hadn't I? How hard could it be to get to the second floor?

Some of my bravado wore off when I reached the main stairway, where a tall automaton stood motionless. It was right in the middle of the third step, effectively blocking the way. But it didn't react as I approached—maybe it wasn't on right now and was only there as a harmless intimidation tactic, like a scarecrow.

Yes, a scarecrow. I liked that analogy. Despite their name, scarecrows didn't frighten me. Not like automatons did. I tried to picture a straw figure instead of a metal contraption covered in bolts and screws with long arms and a rectangular head.

I checked to make sure no one was around, then swung my leg over the railing, intending to climb on the outside of the stair until I passed the automaton.

A loud whirring surprised me so much I nearly lost my grip and toppled to the floor. The automaton's head rotated ninety degrees until its beady red eyes locked on me. "This area is not for guests. Please return to the party."

Its monotone voice sent a shiver down my back, but I laughed sheepishly and took my leg off the railing. "My apologies. I was looking for the restroom. Do you happen to know the way?"

The automaton lifted its left arm and pointed down the hall. "In that direction, you'll find the powder room. It has facilities for both male and female guests. Do you need a guide?"

I waved my hands. "No, no, that won't be necessary. I actually already tried the restroom down there, but it is full. I was hoping to find one upstairs."

"That area is not for guests," it repeated.

I crossed my arms. That answer would have stumped the old Rupert, but I wasn't going to give up so easily. "Except, this is a party, and you are obligated to accommodate me, correct?"

"Affirmative."

"I don't find it very accommodating when I'm not provided with basic necessities. If I complain to the Actons that you're negligent in your duties, will they have you replaced?"

"They will have me checked for damage, and if they find none, they will continue to use me as they see fit. If there are damages, they will either have me repaired or destroyed."

This conversation wasn't going the way I wanted it to. I tried again. "Do you want to be destroyed?"

The automaton tilted its head in an almost curious fashion. "I do not want. I only serve."

Frustration bubbled up inside me. This was like talking to a wall. "But you *want* to serve your masters well, don't you?"

"I serve to the best of my capacity. That is what I was designed to do."

I groaned and turned away, running a hand through my hair. "This is hopeless. I—"

My fingers brushed my mask. Oh, right. Automatons recorded the things they saw, but if the only thing this one could see was a masked man . . .

I whirled around and punched the machine in the torso. "Yow," I squealed, pulling back my throbbing hand. I blew on my bleeding knuckles and peered at the automaton, which seemed completely unfazed by my attack. It hadn't even budged.

"How did that do *nothing* to you?" I screeched, more than a little upset. I wasn't the strongest man, but I'd thought my punch would do some damage, or at least knock it off balance.

Maybe I'd have more success with my feet. I swung my leg to the side, aiming for the automaton's lower half. This time, the machine saw the attack coming and blocked my foot with its hands.

My teeth clamped together as pain reverberated up my leg and I fell onto my backside. The automaton returned to its former position. "Please refrain from touching me," it said calmly.

"Oh, you don't like that, do you? Well, I don't like it when you're in my way." I pulled myself to my feet, infuriated now. This scrap of metal wasn't going to thwart my plans. Not when there was evidence to gather. I closed both hands into fists and held them in front of my face, then bounced back and forth on my feet.

A large wrench swung through the air, hitting the automaton on the back of the neck. The machine pitched forward in a heap, steam hissing from its arm joints. It didn't rise.

The person wielding the wrench stood next to the stairs on the left side. He gave me a wide grin. "How about you stop embarrassing yourself now and we go find that study?"

I gaped. "When did you get here, Mr. Woodhouse?"

The old man chuckled. "Were you so busy you didn't notice me? And here I thought you were distracting it on purpose so I could knock it out."

My gaze returned to the fallen machinery. Though there were no visible signs of damage beyond the steam, Mr. Woodhouse didn't seem worried that it would resume moving anytime soon. "How *did* you do that?"

The old man tucked his wrench into his pocket. "I ought to know how to disarm my own work, don't you think?"

My eyes lit up with understanding. Ah, so that was how he knew the Actons. "Well, thank you for your assistance. I really should be going now."

I started up the stairs, but Woodhouse grabbed my arm. "If you want to get in and out before the Actons figure out what you've done, you're going to need my help. So, why don't you give me that?"

"Give you what?"

The old man scoffed. "The key, of course. These automatons send messages to a main server every thirty minutes to make sure all is well. When this one doesn't report in, it will trigger an alarm that alerts the others. That gives you a very short window of time to find the study. Unless you'd prefer getting arrested?"

"How did you know I was looking for the—" I broke off at his impatient look. "All right, you can tell me later. Here." I handed him the key, praying I wasn't making a mistake in trusting him.

Woodhouse smiled and led me up to the second floor. We went down a long corridor and stopped at the last door. "Here we are." He stuck the key in the keyhole and turned it.

With a soft click, the door opened to a large room with a desk, bookcase, and chairs. A chandelier hung above the desk, illuminating the space with artificial light, and several cabinets stood against the wall. A shiny brass lamp sat atop the desk, along with a few pens and neatly stacked papers.

Woodhouse gestured to the cabinets. "I believe what you're looking for is in there."

I wasted no time in asking how he knew that. Just like when we'd been at Sky Manor, this man knew far more than he should have. I was glad he seemed to be on my side this time, though I couldn't forget the aghast look on his face when I'd locked him out of the automaton workshop just before I'd blown up the manor.

I threw open the cabinets, eyes widening at the sight of film cans. Just like Camilla had said. The only problem was . . . there were six of them. How could I know which was the right one?

"Hurry up," Mr. Woodhouse urged from his spot by the door. "We're almost out of time."

I grabbed all six and shoved them into the hidden pocket inside my cloak, glad the disks were small enough to easily transport. "Let's go."

Woodhouse pulled the door, but it opened to a well-dressed gentleman on the other side.

"Good evening," Wes said smoothly. His smile was malicious, gloating. He slithered into the room like a snake, looking first at Woodhouse, then settling on me. "You weren't trying to steal from me, were you, Rupert?"

Chapter Fifteen

Camilla

Heart pounding, I retrieved my pistol and dove to Horace's side. Regardless of the desk lamp, the dark corners of the room made it impossible to see clearly. Blood soaked into the dress fabric, leaving a deep, incriminating stain across my knees. "Stay with me." I clamped my hands around his face. Tears raced down my nose. "You can't die. I'll get a doctor."

"No," he said. His eyelids cracked open, and he let out a hoarse sigh. "She. Took. The. Evidence."

"Who is *she*?" I asked much too harshly and tried to pivot. "No, I'll call a doctor."

I got to my feet, and a flick of light glistened from the far corner. Hands shaking, I lifted my pistol. I curled my index finger over the hard edge of the trigger.

"You're much too impulsive, little flower," said a gritty female voice. A light glowed, and smoke drifted from the darkness. "Did you think you could get away from the Elite with no repercussions?"

Inside the deep shadows, a woman pushed herself up from the armchair. Leveling my gun, I secured my aim toward the target.

"If you kill me, you'll be accused of double homicide." She tossed the cigarette onto the hardwood section of the floor. A black boot smothered the flame before she retrieved it. "I don't want to leave too much evidence."

Fear struck me harder than the fall from the brick wall at Wes's estate. Even if Wes couldn't accuse me of murder before, now there was a mountain of evidence suggesting I'd shot Horace. Blood coated the bottom of my white dress, and people had seen me escape with Horace—the poor, innocent boy.

The older woman shifted closer to the light, now revealing her harsh face, short hair, and tattoos snaking up her neck. "I just wanted to see if the Camilla Carranza lived up to the newspaper articles printed about her. You are a little flower, aren't you? My son might have chosen the wrong girl."

My head cocked to the side, giving her the second she needed to bolt for the door. I squeezed the trigger. The force of the shot pulsed up my arm and sent a booming noise throughout the quiet estate. Whoever this woman was, I couldn't let her get away. She had killed—no, he wasn't dead yet—wounded Horace, and she had the evidence proving my innocence. I threw off my heels and sprinted out of the door.

"What was that?" the butler shouted.

"Get a medic. A woman shot Horace." I scrambled around the corner and followed the stranger through a doorway. My heavy mask shifted over the bridge of my nose, but I couldn't slow down to rip it off.

This time, the room had no light besides the open window at the other end. The silhouette of the woman jumping from the open window disappeared into the night. I closed in on her, but by the time I peered below, she was leaping off a portico and into the night. A dizzy spell overtook me at the great height, but after what she'd done, I climbed out of the window, prayed under my breath, and jumped onto a lower roof and then the portico. My mask slipped a fraction upward.

Rage pounded at my temples. This woman deserved to pay for her crimes. I couldn't let her go without repercussions. She continued through the estate gardens like a streak of darkness, barely visible. I vaulted off the portico, shaken by the fall but powered by my need to catch her.

Chapter Sixteen

Rupert

"I don't know what you're talking about," I stammered once I could formulate a response. Sweat pooled down my back as Wes peered at me, amusement twitching at his lips.

"Oh, don't you?" He strolled inside, one hand in his trouser pocket. I remained behind the desk, trying to subtly scan the room for another exit. The large window on my left seemed to be the only other potential escape route, but jumping from this height was liable to result in a broken limb, or worse.

"Tell me, then," Wes continued, "who else would be stupid enough to steal from me?" He inclined his head toward Mr. Woodhouse, who'd retreated to a nearby corner where a bust rested on a small table. "And choose someone as obvious as Sky Manor's old butler to be his accomplice?"

I clenched my jaw. "I'm sure there are plenty of people who'd like to steal from you. What exactly *is* on these films?"

Wes paled, fear sparking in his eyes before it disappeared behind the suave swagger I knew all too well. He stepped toward me and opened his palm. "How about you hand those over, and we can forget this ever happened?"

A fuzzy feeling came over me as I reached inside the hidden pocket of my cloak. This evening had gone from bad to worse. Wouldn't it be nice to just forget about all of it?

"Don't do it, Rupert," Woodhouse murmured, low enough that Wes couldn't make out his words.

My hand froze, something like fog dissipating from my brain. Why was I about to give Wes the films? That was the exact *opposite* of what I wanted to do.

I internally winced as I recalled Wes's blessing. His ability to sway people wasn't foolproof, as evidenced by Woodhouse's successful intervention, but it had landed me in plenty of dangerous and sometimes downright embarrassing situations over the years. *Rupert, you fool, how could you fall for that same old trick again?*

Wes was still waiting for me to comply. His mouth stretched into a broad grin even as his left eye twitched with impatience.

I moved my hand away from the films and met his gaze squarely. My days of being threatened were over. "I have a better idea. You step aside, and we walk out of here with the films. Whatever we find on them, we'll keep it to ourselves, and in return, you won't mess with Camilla again."

Wes let out a short, disappointed sigh, making a tuft of blond hair float upward before settling back against his forehead. "I'd hoped I wouldn't need to resort to this." He clapped his hands, and an automaton appeared in the doorway. While its basic form was the same as the one from the staircase, this one was much broader, and it had two glowing red canisters attached to its elbows. It rolled into the room on two wheels and turned to await its master's instructions.

I gulped, not liking the looks of this. Most automatons were used for elementary functions, like delivering messages and cleaning, but the liquid sloshing around in those canisters reminded me very much of the radioactive green ooze at Sky Manor.

"Execute Protocol 659," Wes ordered, satisfaction gleaming in his blue eyes. He stepped around the machine to leave the room.

Woodhouse grabbed the bust off the table and lobbed it at the doorway. It hit Wes's skull with a sickening crack, and down he went, blood dripping from his temple.

"You stupid wretch, I'm going to—"

The automaton cut off Wes's tirade as it rolled over the top of his legs. Wes howled in agony, then fell unconscious. The automaton, nonplussed by its master's situation, continued its approach, stopping just in front of the desk. It lifted its arms, and suddenly the canisters swirled, stirring the liquid within.

I didn't know what Protocol 659 was, but I wasn't going to wait around to find out. When Woodhouse jumped over Wes's prone form and hurried out of the open doorway, I was quick to follow. Except, instead of trying to avoid Wes, I stomped over him with more force than necessary.

Before I could get down the hallway, something grabbed hold of my ankle, wrenching me to the floor. I leaned back and came face to face with Wes, who wasn't as unconscious as I'd hoped.

He gave me a crazed smile. "Wait up, Rupert. Don't want you to miss the grand finale."

I kicked at my assailant, but he pulled a dagger from his coat sleeve and jammed it through the edge of my cloak into the floor. When I tried to move, the material didn't tear, and I nearly choked myself. If I was going to escape, this cloak wasn't coming with me.

Meanwhile, Wes had pushed himself up from his stomach and was rising on shaky legs.

"What are you up to now?" I snarled, trying not to panic when the automaton's canisters stopped spinning and the nozzles on top of its arms rotated in my direction.

"Last chance, Rupert," Wes warned. "Give me the films, or you won't like what's coming." He held out his hand.

I shook my head. No matter how much charm he infused into his words, I wasn't going to be fooled again. Camilla's freedom depended on it. "I don't have them. Woodhouse does."

Wes scowled. "Then you leave me with no choice." He moved his hand to a ring on his left forefinger. A bright red stone sat in its center, surrounded by sparkling white diamonds. He pressed the middle stone, which began pulsating with light.

"Say goodbye to your girlfriend."

My blood turned to ice. *What have I done?*

"Of course," Wes continued, a malicious glint in his eye, "you'll be joining her soon enough." He stumbled over to the door and pulled it shut behind him. The click that followed was so soft it was almost inaudible, yet the sound sent a tremor through me.

I was locked in.

The automaton beeped, then released two streams of red gas that spread over the room like fiery mist. I held my breath and turned away, struggling to undo the clasp on my cloak.

I was starting to get dizzy from the lack of oxygen, but I forced myself not to breathe. Camilla needed me. Just as my fingers unfastened the cloak, the door creaked open. My head snapped up, taking in a vaguely human shape.

"Rupert, let's go!" came Woodhouse's voice. He grabbed my arms, hauling me to my feet.

I checked over my shoulder. The automaton was still spreading the noxious fumes in a wide arc, but when it spotted the old man, it swung toward him. Woodhouse's eyes widened, and he pushed me into the hallway just before the automaton gave him a full blast of hot gas.

The old man bent over, coughing and hacking up blood. I moved to help him, but he waved for me to go on, sputtering something about rescuing Camilla, and dug his wrench out of his coat pocket.

The jaws bore a blood stain that hadn't been there before. Something in my gut told me whose it was. "Did you . . . ?"

The old man's eyes flashed, answering the question I hadn't dared voice. "I'll buy you some time," he promised. Before I realized what he was doing, he'd slammed the door, closing himself in with the automaton.

I tried to open the door, but it wouldn't budge. I banged on it desperately. "Woodhouse! Woodhouse!"

Gas seeped under the crack, spilling into the hall. I covered my mouth and leaped back. Leaving the old man went against my instincts, but I couldn't let his sacrifice be in vain. Wes may be gone, but his final act could have cost Camilla everything.

I dashed down the corridor, praying harder than I ever had.

CHAPTER SEVENTEEN

Camilla

MY MASK SLIPPED FARTHER down, a hindrance to catching Horace's shooter. I yanked it off with one hand and threw it to the side.

The wall exploded. Through flames, I could make out Horace's mansion catching fire. Bricks and debris shot at me from whatever the blast had ignited within the mansion. I pushed off the ground, searching the darkness, but upon pushing up, my head swam. I must have hit my head against the cement harder than I'd realized.

A distant cackle echoed from afar in the same grated voice of the murderer. I'd lost her, and I'd lost Horace.

If I could reverse time, I would. I hobbled to the crumbling wall and found a small electrical device in the shape of what once was my mask. Wes had planned to get rid of me from the start.

I stepped back and let out a long breath. Temptation to join Wes's twisted game had lured me in because my need for riches and fame had trapped me again. A warm tear slithered down my cheek with the unbidden wash of emotion.

No matter what happened next, I had to let Rupert know about what I'd done. The only gain from the entire night would be that I'd identified who was behind the Games. It brought little comfort when all the power tipped in Wes Acton's family's favor.

Keeping to the shadows, I hobbled through the night, aware of the throbbing lump on my head, my scabbed-over hands, and my sore knees. But I managed to cross the city to the one place I should have gone first.

The small estate stood in a row of modest tenements, lit by the occasional gas lamp on the streets. I climbed the half-dozen steps and prayed under my breath for Rupert to answer my call.

I tapped the door with my scraped knuckles, careful not to awaken the neighbors. A rustle sounded behind me. My heart leapt, and I whipped around to find a cat out for a midnight stroll.

"Cursed feline," I mumbled under my shaky breath.

The door locks clanked. *Oh, bless Rupert for being such a light sleeper*, I thought to myself. I huddled close to the handle, ready to push in the moment the door opened.

Fingers wrapped around my wrist and yanked me inside. My gaze drifted from the black vest to the buttons fastening the cloak around the man's neck. The pale face of someone who was not Rupert met my eye.

"You!" I shouted.

CHAPTER EIGHTEEN

Camilla

ZENITH SLAMMED THE FRONT door shut. "Did anyone follow you?" His cold manner and smooth movements from the foyer to the parlor curtains to check outside the windows rang of someone practiced in working with the underbelly of society.

Though Rupert's darkened foyer hadn't any light, the familiar place eased the knot of panic inside my chest enough for me to catch my breath. Rupert had spoken of meeting Zenith at the Screaming Peach Café, and Maple, my tentative friend, spoke highly of Zenith. If they trusted him, I should restrain myself from pulling out my pistol. He wasn't the enemy.

"No one followed," I said. "I think the lady got away."

"Which lady?" He paced along the parlor windows, allowing a stream of street light to catch the hard edges of his serious face. Though he'd proven himself somewhat trustworthy compared to the other Sky Manor contestants, I retreated from him.

I stepped into the parlor so I could keep my voice pitched low, as if describing her might manifest the wretched soul. "It was an older woman with a snake tattoo on her neck. I think Wes hired her."

Someone knocked on the front door. Then the sound of metal jingled on the other side of the door. Instinctively, I hid behind Zenith and reached for my pistol.

Zenith flipped the switch, turning on the front lights, and opened the front door.

Rupert sighed with relief and bent over in the doorway of his house. His perfect hair swept to each side of his face, but dark circles lay beneath his feverish eyes.

I looked down at my dress, now ripped and splattered with blood. How must I look to him?

Zenith righted himself from his heavy lean against the door frame. "Good evening, Rupert. I should go keep an eye on Camilla's family. We'll have to talk about a possible safe house." He patted Rupert's shoulder and made his way out of the front door. The pale pink hue of morning light speared through the clouds in the sky.

"Thank you, friend." Rupert locked the door and slid a metal bold into place. The serious expression hardening my sweet Rupert's face cracked the small semblance of sanity still left in me after the long night. He led me to sit beside him on the parlor couch.

In the morning light, his tan skin glowed, and his dark eyes glinted as if a sheen of tears coated them. I could break into a million pieces before him from the guilt and embarrassment of having to admit that I had done the exact opposite of his recommendation and ultimately, had received a heaping spoonful of disaster.

"You went to the masquerade." Rupert's flat tone didn't encourage my tongue to loosen.

I nodded.

"Is that your blood? Did Wes hurt you?"

Tipping my head down to observe the hard crimson stains along the bodice of my white gown, I swallowed at how this might appear to him. He already had his reservations because of how riches had always been my guiding star.

Then, I caught a glimpse of the discoloration on his black trousers. "Is that blood?"

"It's Mister Woodhouse's."

"Is he . . ." I couldn't get my mouth to form the word.

Rupert whispered, "He's gone."

My tears flowed freely along my nose, over my lips, and off my chin. The old butler from the mansion was dead? Confusion lodged in my throat like someone had stuffed a rock inside to suffocate me. How was he, of all people, gone?

"He protected me from Wes."

Sobs escaped, and I slapped my hand over my mouth to keep them from taking over, but my whole body shook. First, Horace and now, Mister Woodhouse. Strong arms wrapped around my torso, and I pressed my cheek onto his shoulder, unable to meet his gaze. We'd never be safe again, and two people had lost their lives because of my failures. For the duration of my tears, he held me, which inspired another tumble of sobs because why did he have to be so good?

Once I'd run out of energy to weep, I stared at the hardwood floor and leaned on Rupert's shoulder, realizing that all my dreams might be lost. Though I'd kept my mask on most of the time, Horace's maid and butler might accuse me of murder, and so might Horace's family. Then there was the matter of Lady Arabella threatening my family. We'd all have to move. Rupert's lack of a proposal would be the least of my troubles.

Rupert pulled away and slid his hand along my cheek, encouraging me to meet his gaze. But I kept my eyes on his thumb and the yellow walls, anywhere but at Rupert.

"Please, Camilla, you know I adore you and would like the opportunity to understand what happened to you last night." He shifted to try to get me to look at him.

I closed my eyes and covered his hand on his cheek with mine. His warmth and comfort coaxed me to finally look at him, and what I saw was furrowed eyebrows and concern rather than accusation.

So, I did. I told him every last detail, down to the lace on Lady Anabella's mask and the dreadful dance with Dunstan.

"We're not free from the Sky Manor," I said.

"I destroyed it. It's no more, Camilla. They can't force us to go to their new game."

"Mister Woodhouse told me that he'd been asked to be caretaker again for the new game and heard plans to have all of us participate. They're out for revenge; I just know it. You destroyed their investment. I didn't fall in line. The city council believes there are riches to be made, and our only ally might concede with his son dead."

Rupert leaned back in his chair and raked his fingers through his thick hair. "What if I told you that Wes won't be bothering us anymore?"

I cocked my head to the side. Rupert dug in his suit jacket and produced an iron mask. When he placed the dark metal over his face, I gasped.

CHAPTER NINETEEN

Rupert

CAMILLA'S SOFT INTAKE OF breath pierced me like a dagger. Would she even want to be with me anymore now that she knew I'd fooled her?

I swallowed thickly and risked a glance at her eyes. To my shock, they weren't overcome with rage, just confusion. Maybe I could still get out of this. Yes, I could lie and tell her I'd found the mask outside and—

My prayer from the hedge maze came back to haunt me. The man Camilla deserved was brave enough to be honest with her. And that meant confessing my sins, no matter the consequences.

I ran my fingers over the cool metal of the mask, trying to anchor myself before I plunged in headfirst. "I went to your house last night, but when your mother told me you weren't there, I knew there was only one place you could have gone," I started. "I went to fetch you, but the Actons' automaton wouldn't let me into the manor without an invitation, so I had to . . . improvise."

"Improvise," Camilla echoed, a hint of bitterness in her tone. Her hands were clasped tightly in the folds of her dress, as if she were just barely keeping herself from punching me.

I winced. This wasn't a good start. "I wanted to—"

"To find out if I was messing around behind your back, right?" Her voice was all bite now, cracking at the end like she was trying not to cry.

"Right?" she said again when I didn't reply.

"Yes," I admitted, though the confession tasted like ash in my mouth. Shame weighed down my shoulders. "I was a coward of the worst kind. I understand if you don't want anything to do with me anymore, but . . . these are for you."

I reached into my pocket and pulled out the film cans.

Camilla's brown eyes were as big as dinner plates. "Are those . . . ?"

I nodded as I handed them over, feeling a flicker of satisfaction. At least I'd done one thing right by her. Maybe eventually she'd find it in her heart to forgive me. "The footage Wes used to blackmail you. I got it."

"You already knew about that? From when you were roaming around in that horrible mask?"

I started to nod again, but her gaze sharpened, a wrinkle forming between her perfect eyebrows.

"Tell me everything," she said.

I sighed. It was only fair. I laid out my version of the evening, sharing what I'd overheard, how I'd followed her through the maze, the fight with Wes that had resulted in both his and Mr. Woodhouse's deaths, even my brief encounter with Zenith's mom, whom I now realized I never should have let out of my sight. When I finished, I felt a bit lighter, but the dread coiling in my gut remained.

Because now that she knew everything, she had no reason to stay.

She didn't speak for a long time, but when she finally did, she asked, "What about the other films? Are all of these from Sky Manor?"

"I don't think so. I haven't gotten a chance to look at them yet, but based on Wes's reaction, I'm guessing there's something on here we can use against the game makers—I . . . I mean you. *You* can use it against them. Or at the very least, the films should offer you some protection so they don't come after you again. I already explained everything to Zenith, and he's going to get some of his contacts to keep an eye on Lady Arabella to make sure she doesn't send anyone after us."

I folded my hands together, trying to keep myself from crying. I'd blown it, but at least Camilla would be safe now. That should be enough for me.

Camilla's hand touched the top of mine.

I lifted my head in confusion.

"Do you still keep the popcorn in the cupboard on the right?" She winked. "Don't look so stummed."

"Do you mean stumped?"

"You know what I mean. I meant it when I said I loved you." A long, glorious moment passed in her meaningful gaze. "We're going to need some popcorn for all those films."

"But . . ." Conflict stilled my tongue. "I should take you home. Your parents will be worried about you."

"This is *for* my parents and everyone the game makers might use against us. We're never going back to those games of fortune and tomfoolery." She waved a hand to mark the end of our conversation and the end of my doubts.

I watched speechlessly as my future wife poured popcorn into a pan. Never had a lady been more beautiful than in that moment as the aroma of butter and sound of popping corn filled the air.

If you enjoyed
Of Masquerades and Fame,
consider reading the rest of
the Games of Greed and Ruin series.

BOOK 1

BOOK 2

Camilla and Rupert will return in the next installment of the series.

Follow the authors here:

Acknowledgments

Thank you so much to our loving families for their support and encouragement as we put in the time, effort, and creativity needed to bring this story to life. Creating a book is no easy feat, and with the many other demands on our energy and time, we appreciate how our families stepped us to allow us the margin needed to make *Of Masquerades and Fame* a reality.

Thank you to our wonderful beta readers, whose comments were hilarious, motivating, and insightful. We not only channeled our inner fire swamp and inner Hannah Lucero, but we also fixed up several plot holes thanks to your great input.

Thank you to Selina De Luca for utilizing your hawk eyes as our proofreader and finding those hard-to-spot errors. You even found Camilla's misuse of the word "defiantly," which was so funny since it was an intentional mistake from our favorite pistol-wielding heroine.

Thank you also to each other. It's great to have a partner for brainstorming, marketing, and leaning into each other's strengths. Camilla and Rupert are so much fun, but having someone to share in the joy of creating their stories made the experience even better.

And none of it would be possible without Christ gifting us with the ideas and energy needed to make this happen. May our words and actions please You, and we pray You continue to use these stories for Your glory and the sanctification of Your people.

About the Author

Candice Pedraza Yamnitz fell in love with *The Lord of the Rings* and *Pride and Prejudice* in high school and hasn't stopped reading since. She taught in a dual-language elementary classroom for years until she decided to stay at home, teaching a crew of imaginative children. In between reading lessons and converting cardboard boxes into pirate ships, she writes YA novels with a Latin twist. She lives in her native Chicagoland. Visit her at candiceyamnitz.com and find her on Instagram and TikTok at @candiceyamnitz.

Also By Candice...

UNBETROTHED
UNTAMED
ASSASSINS RISE
DESSI AND KY GO POOF
DEAR MOUSE PRINCESS

About the Author

Claire Kohler is a North Carolina author with a penchant for rich historical settings, heart-wrenching romance, and dazzling creatures. She writes clean historical romantasy that's immersive, meaningful, and compelling. She is also an editor and tutor. When she's not working, you'll find her homeschooling her children, bingeing Korean dramas with her husband, and leading Bible studies at her church. Connect with her at http://www.clairekohlerbooks.com or on Instagram and TikTok at @clairekohlerbooks.

Also By Claire...

GUMIHO KISS

THE SECRET OF DRULEA COTTAGE

THE HEART OF EVERTON INN

THE TREASURE OF RIGMORE HOUSE